The Heav'n Rescued Land

9/14/2016 Frank

Frank Becker

Greenbush Press

Spring, TX

Copyright © 2014, 2016 by Frank Becker

E-book published simultaneously worldwide.

Becker, Frank
Series: "The Chronicles of CC"

Book Two
The Heav'n Rescued Land / Frank Becker

ISBN:
Paperback, 978-0-9836460-5-1
Electronic Book, 978-0-9836460-8-2

Library of Congress Control Number (LCCN): 2013955691

Fiction: Christian, Action-adventure, Inspirational, Futuristic

Printed in the United States of America

This is a work of fiction. Names, characters, places, and incidents either are the product of the author's imagination or are used fictitiously, and any resemblance to actual persons, living or dead, businesses, companies, events, or locales is entirely coincidental.

The Heav'n Rescued Land

is for

Pastor Joe and Donna Flynn

The Star Spangled Banner
Francis Scott Key, 1814

Oh, say can you see by the dawn's early light
What so proudly we hailed at the twilight's last gleaming?
Whose broad stripes and bright stars thru the perilous fight,
O'er the ramparts we watched were so gallantly streaming?
And the rocket's red glare, the bombs bursting in air,
Gave proof through the night that our flag was still there.
Oh, say does that star-spangled banner yet wave
O'er the land of the free and the home of the brave?

On the shore, dimly seen through the mists of the deep,
Where the foe's haughty host in dread silence reposes,
What is that which the breeze, o'er the towering steep,
As it fitfully blows, half conceals, half discloses?
Now it catches the gleam of the morning's first beam,
In full glory reflected now shines in the stream:
'Tis the star-spangled banner! Oh long may it wave
O'er the land of the free and the home of the brave!

And where is that band who so vauntingly swore
That the havoc of war and the battle's confusion,
A home and a country should leave us no more!
Their blood has washed out their foul footsteps' pollution.
No refuge could save the hireling and slave
From the terror of flight, or the gloom of the grave:
And the star-spangled banner in triumph doth wave
O'er the land of the free and the home of the brave!

Oh! thus be it ever, when freemen shall stand
Between their loved home and the war's desolation!
Blest with victory and peace, may the heav'n rescued land
Praise the Power that hath made and preserved us a nation.
Then conquer we must, when our cause it is just,
And this be our motto: "In God is our trust."
And the star-spangled banner in triumph shall wave
O'er the land of the free and the home of the brave!

"...and this desire on my part, exempt from all vanity of authorship, had for its only object and hope that it might be useful to others as a lesson of morality, patience, courage, perseverance, and Christian submission to the will of God."

—Johann Wyss, 1812, author,
The Swiss Family Robinson

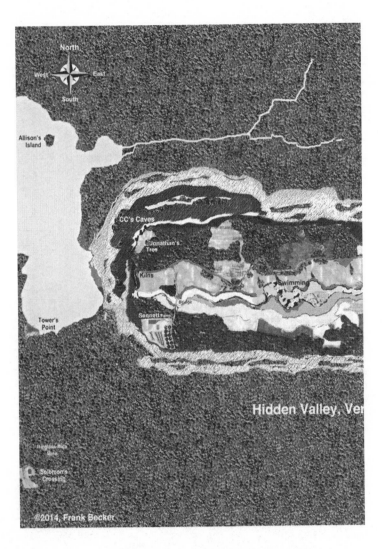

West End, Hidden Valley

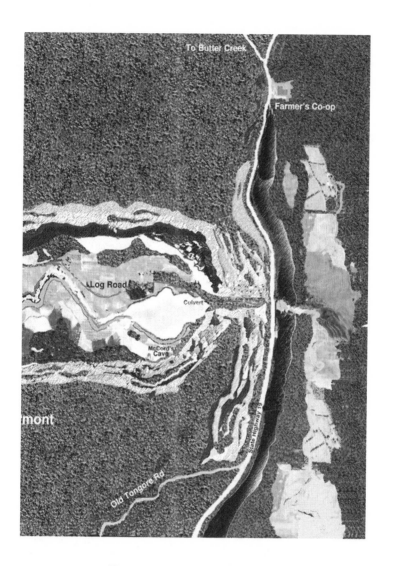

East End, Hidden Valley

The Promised Land

Hidden Valley, Vermont
May 9th, 7:32 p.m.

CC stopped in mid-stride, almost tripping over his feet as his eyes took in the scene before him. Darkness surrounded him, but just ahead sunlight spilled through the end of the narrow ravine, turning the trees into a mass of translucent golds, greens and blues.

Huge oaks stood off to either side, their branches intertwined high above his head. Yet, when his eyes swept the ground around him, he realized he was walking along a narrow lane that was clear of trees and underbrush — covered only with a thick layer of leaves.

Amazement turned to excitement. Now that he had discovered this narrow defile splitting the cliffs, it was as if the setting sun was beckoning him on. For a moment he wondered whether it was welcoming him to a new hope, or enticing him on to fatal disappointment?

A few hundred paces further along, he heard the sound of flowing water. Although he'd entered through a narrow ravine, he now found himself entering a much wider valley. As he left the cover of the trees, he discovered himself overlooking a small lake. He looked to the far side, and discovered that it was fed by a stream flowing in from the valley beyond. The lake covered about eight acres of the valley floor immediately in front and to his left. The trail he'd been following curved around its right side.

When he reached the edge of the lake, he found himself standing atop a moss-covered stone dam or retaining wall. Carefully leaning out over its edge, he found himself staring down into the opening of an enormous culvert pipe.

He laughed aloud. He'd discovered the source of the stream that flowed beneath the highway. Turning abruptly, he raced back toward his truck, concerned because it was parked in plain view on the highway beneath the cliffs that hid the entrance to this amazing valley.

He stopped to kick at the layer of composting leaves beneath his feet and, to his further surprise, discovered that they hid the remains of a crumbling macadam road. The pungent odor of rotting vegetation evoked thoughts of hiking and camping, and suggested the isolated sort of environment which he had been seeking.

CC wasn't going to take time to ponder why this abandoned road and the huge pipe beneath it existed. His curiosity, and maybe something more, had brought him a great opportunity. Now he needed to capitalize on the potential.

If it was not already too late, if the tractor-trailer had not already been spotted by the pilot of the low-flying plane, he had to get the rig into this narrow canyon before it was noticed, for undoubtedly the aircraft was operated by one or another of America's invaders.

He stopped beneath the branches of the tall evergreens that bordered the highway, and threw a glance in the direction in which he'd last seen the light aircraft. It was no longer in sight. It was his intention to get the truck off the highway and move it as far as possible up this narrow canyon. Knowing that time was against him, he made a quick estimate of the distance between the larger of the trees, and gauged with his eyes the likelihood of driving the tractor-trailer between them. If he were able to get it into the valley, he suspected that it would remain there forever.

With his limited experience driving such a rig, there seemed only the smallest chance that he'd make it, but he also knew that he would never find a better hideaway. Driving that huge truck between those trees appeared more difficult to him than getting a camel through the eye of a needle, but whether he might succeed or not, his circumstances compelled him to try. In the gathering darkness, he quickly surveyed the path he would follow.

He wondered briefly what natural forces had created this improbable gap in the mountain wall, but could not afford the luxury of time to dwell on the question.

A geologist might have told him that long ago enormous forces of fire and pressure from within the earth's core had twisted the amorphous mass near the surface, resulting in a radical dip in the mountains, an anticline, and that the bottom of that cleft had formed a box canyon through which the mountain stream had tumbled. He might also have argued that the stream took thousands of years to cut its way down through the rock, reshaping the valley until, in the recent past, the engineers had redirected the stream's path.

CC realized that he would argue over the time required to accomplish such work. He'd visited Mount St. Helens before and after the volcanic eruption, and knew what seemingly impossible changes can be made to the surface of the earth in mere hours. It had torn apart a mountain, changed the lives of thousands, and transformed millions of acres of pristine forest into a virtual wasteland. And then another thought intruded. *The Book states that God created the world in six days. Period!*

One thing seemed certain. CC might never learn how the valley was formed, or why the engineers had diverted the stream to churn its way through the culvert pipe beneath his feet, but he did know that it might enable him to escape from the open highway into that hidden valley.

Just In Time

Hidden Valley
Rt 19, Central Vermont
May 9th, 7:58 p.m.

His chest was still heaving, the result of running while wearing a lead X-ray apron and breathing through a nuisance dust mask. Realizing that he could not save the truck while worrying about the radiation count, he slipped out of the vest, let it drop beneath the trees, and again took off running toward the truck.

As he neared the road, he again took note of the broad shallow ditch that the highway's builders had dug along the highway's edge to carry off rainwater. This swale ran parallel to the highway and cut across the end of the hidden lane that he needed to enter. It didn't simply disguise the old log road, it effectively severed it from the highway. He was doubtful that he could drive the overloaded rig across, but he was determined to try.

Running back to the truck, CC caught a glimpse of the plane returning to the crossroads far up the valley. He had shut the engine down to conserve fuel. Now, as he pulled himself up into the cab, he thought of the maddening seconds he might have to wait to preheat the big diesel. He cranked up the compressed air and hit the starter. It exploded into operation, catching on the first try. Breathing a prayer of thanks, he slammed it into reverse and backed up so violently that he almost jackknifed the trailer into the stone retaining wall.

Pulling the wheel around hand over hand, he cut the tractor across the uphill lane, gunning the engine hard as he approached the ditch at nearly a ninety degree angle. The tractor careened down into the swale and the front wheels began to plow the thin layer of muck at the bottom. The engine seemed to fade a little as it lost torque, but then began to roar again, and he felt power surging to the drive axles.

The rig slowed frighteningly as the wheels dug in, but the weight of the trailer saved him. Just as he thought the tractor would bog down and stop, the momentum of that heavy trailer pushed the back axle of the tractor down and forward, bouncing the front wheels of the cab up and out of the ditch onto firmer ground.

Uncertain what to do, he kept the pedal on the floor, hoping to avoid fish-tailing. Time seemed to stand still as the tractor's rear wheels spun in the mud, then slowly began to inch their way up out of the swale. He again thought he was defeated when the rear of the cab began to slide sideways and the rig began to jackknife. If it slid too far, he'd smash the side of the trailer into the trees or hang it up in the ditch.

It was a close thing, but the tractor's eight drive wheels with their brand new tires suddenly caught, and the load be-gan to creep forward again. Then the eight wheels supporting the rear of the trailer, over fifty feet behind him, hit the low spot in the swale and started to dig in. The drag on the wheels jerked the tractor and trailer back into a straight line.

By now the engine was screaming so loudly that CC thought it might throw a rod. The drive wheels were spinning, but the truck was only creeping forward. Afraid to try to shift gears because he might stall the engine or blow out the trans-mission, he simply kept his foot on the accelerator. The back wheels of the trailer hit the uphill bank of the swale with a bounce, cleared the worse spot, started to slip sideways again, leveled off, and cleared the ditch.

Even in the midst of the truck's almost uncontrollable career, CC was thinking of the fuel being gulped down by that roaring engine. He began to let up on the pedal as the cab roared between the last two tall hemlocks that stood in the shadow of the cliff. The truck was now slightly askew the desired path, but CC kept the drive wheels turning as fast as he could in low gear without allowing them to spin. The steering wheel was jerking back and forth in his hands, and his foot jounced up and down on the accelerator pedal as the truck bounced over the uneven ground. Pine boughs were slapping against the windshield, and he could barely see where he was going.

Risking the possibility that the pilot of that plane might spot the rig beneath the trees, he reached out with his left hand and turned on the headlights. A glance back in his west coast mirror showed that the side of the trailer about to drag against a tree on the left side, and he floored the pedal. The rig again straightened out, but the trailer scraped against a broken limb, making a deep crease along its upper side. *Why,* he wondered, *did that make me think of the iceberg that tore the life from the hull of the Titanic?*

That random thought fled as the rig pulled free, passing deeper into the shadows of the narrow pass, rolling over tiny saplings like some Brobdingnagian giant as he steered toward the water gate. In spite of the crawling pace of the wheels, the jarring movement of the vehicle through the twilit underbrush made the movements seem both precipitous and frightening.

The idyllic little lake flashed into view, captured in the sweep of the headlight's beams. Beyond it he saw the stream that fed the lake, the water dancing in the sunset where it careened over rocks and ledges before pouring into the lake. Even though he was several hundred yards away, he could see that the stream was dizzying in its motion. He steered to the right, turning away from the end of the lake where the water gathered before it poured into the culvert pipe.

The left front wheel of his tractor was now perilously close to the retaining wall where the culvert pipe opened, and, as it passed beyond the wall, the eroding bank began to crumble under the heavy trailer's wheels. Turning in a few feet, he drew the rig to a stop, turned off the lights, set the brake, shut down the engine, and sat there shaking with excitement and fatigue.

He realized, he had no time to rest. Leaping from the cab, he made a lumbering run for the highway, now several hundred yards behind him. His breath came in gasping wheezes, and he realized that if he hoped to survive he would have to carefully marshall his strength. He fought the sense of panic which resulted from oxygen deprivation, then gave up and ripped off the nuisance dust mask in order to breathe easier. Though he knew that the air might contain radioactive dust, the cool evening air tasted delicious.

As he neared the road, he looked around for the marks of his truck's passing. He hoped to scrape away any signs of the telltale tire tracks with a fallen branch, but the ground was firm and rocky, and there was little sign of his movement.

The muddy drainage ditch beside the road contained tire markings, so he used a fallen limb to try to smear the mud around. That served to do little more than coat his shoes with the sticky substance, so he made two trips back into to the woods to scoop up armfuls of dry leaves and pour them over the tire tracks. Then he threw some fallen branches onto the leaves. He could only hope that a rainstorm would soon wash away any sign of his passing.

He ducked back into the trees just as he heard the engine of the search plane passing overhead. Evidently the pilot had cut back his throttle to mask the sound of his approach. A bull-horn blared as the plane banked, sliding off its port wingtip to glide out across the valley. A coarse voice was cursing, and the plane was almost past when CC heard the threat, "Get to town, or we'll carry you there in a body bag."

CC was shaken by the threat, but he wondered whether the pilot was bluffing. He suspected that he frequently shouted warnings like that in order to flush out hidden refugees, and he was reasonably sure that he had not seen the truck. If he had, CC figured he wouldn't have shouted a warning, but would have called for reinforcements on the ground. He realized that, sooner or later, other searchers would come this way.

As the plane disappeared, he took out his little LED flashlight to examine his repair work. He noticed that the bent grass and shrubs were already straightening up, so he turned and jogged back into the woods.

Picking up the lead vest, he walked on to where he'd left the truck, shining his flashlight here and there. He was surprised to see a weathered sign hanging from a tree that read,

"Hidden Valley." Below it was a faded paper sign, "Private Property, No Trespassing."

The Sneakers

Rt 19, Central Vermont
May 9th, 8:05 PM

McCord had already become annoyed with himself for picking up a damsel in distress. He had become even more uncomfortable when her initial fear of riding on the back of the motorcycle caused her to press against his back to keep herself balanced. Since then he'd found himself barely able to tolerate her presence.

Now, as he cleared the top of a hill on State Road 19, he was even more annoyed because she slapped his arm to get his attention.

If I have to stop one more time for this girl to run behind a tree, he thought, *I'll take off and leave her behind.*

Just in time he realized that she was pointing out across the valley, and when his eyes followed her pointing finger, he saw a small plane turning in their general direction.

Wasting no time, he hit the breaks, causing the bike to skid sideways as he rode it under the trees on the left side of the road. Shutting the engine down, they dismounted and stood under the cover of the trees, hoping they were hidden from view.

He was keeping a careful eye on the plane when she again slapped the sleeve of his leather jacket. Well, to be fair, it was more like an excited pat, but it still upset him. Nonetheless, she'd just saved their necks, so he would condescend to her this one additional time. Now she was pointing down the hill, and as he turned to look, he thought he saw the rear end of a truck disappear into the trees on the left side of the road, just a few hundred yards from where they stood.

"Did you see what I saw?" the woman asked.

"If you thought you saw a big truck, yeah, I guess I did too."

They continued to hide beneath the trees, switching their attention between the spot where the truck had disappeared and the path of the oncoming plane. McCord was pre-occupied with the plane, and with good reason. Though still maybe a mile away, it appeared to be heading directly for them.

He pushed the bike behind a large tree, and they huddled together as they continued to watch the plane draw closer. It was obvious that it was an old propeller driven job, and it was moving slowly. A moment later they heard an amplified voice shout, "Get to town, or we'll carry you there in a body bag." The plane moved on, did a slow turn, and headed back up the valley in the rapidly darkening sky.

As soon as he was reasonably sure the plane wouldn't return, the man climbed back on his bike, jumped up and down on the starter, waited for the girl to clamber on behind him, let out the clutch, and kept to the shoulder as he moved slowly downhill. When he found where the truck had left the road, he followed across the swale and up into the trees. Then he again shut down the motor.

Into the Valley

Hidden Valley
Rt 19, Central Vermont
May 9th, 8:10 p.m.

Figuring that the plane would have to return to its base for fuel, and that darkness would keep the pilot from resuming his search until morning, CC decided to pull the truck away from the disintegrating stream bank and onto more solid ground.

This time he didn't have to worry about a fast start, so he was not surprised when he got one. He felt the big engine vibrating through the throttle pedal as he pulled away from the bank. Putting the transmission into the lowest of its sixteen forward gears, he let the clutch out slowly. The big rig jerked forward, then began to crawl ahead.

When someone has driven a vehicle any appreciable distance, they seem to sense as much as see or hear any change in its behavior. CC felt the tractor slow, as though it was dragging an extra burden, and he looked in his side door mirror just in time to see the trailer begin to tip slightly toward the lake, the dirt and gravel sliding away as the bank began to collapse beneath the weight of the four wheels on the trailer's left rear corner.

Slamming the accelerator down, he jerked the steering wheel to the right, trying to get the cab as close to the valley wall as possible. The trailer doggy-walked along with its rear wheels half turning, half sliding along the edge of the bank, churning up mud and water, its tilted rear axles just clearing the ground.

CC felt sure he was losing the rig, and wondered how he'd get clear if the trailer dragged the cab into the lake. The pool which formed at the mouth of that giant pipe looked almost big enough to swallow the entire rig. And if the truck plugged the end of the pipe, the lake would rise, and maybe pour out the mouth of the valley. But that was not his concern. By then he'd almost certainly have drowned.

The tractor itself, having inched clear of the narrow defile, was now on a smoother roadway. The slope of the bank was less steep, and the rear wheels were slowly trailing back up onto the primitive road. Suddenly the truck accelerated ahead, and he realized that the rear wheels had pulled clear of the embankment. The tractors' big drive wheels were now pulling the trailer easily along, and he breathed a prayer of thanks.

After clearing the end of the lake, he continued driving slowly, staying clear of the stream's edge, running the engine smoothly and quietly as he crept along in low gear.

Though it was almost completely dark now, CC could still make out the cliffs looming above him on either side of the valley. The residue of the ages — boulders, gravel, and soil — lay at the base of the cliffs in huge piles. The palisades soared above him, their faces fractured and eroded. Wide steep slopes of broken rock and scree appeared ready to slide down upon him if sufficient shock were to be applied.

He drove on a few hundred yards to where the valley was significantly wider, and the road curved away from the cliffs. Signs of landslides and avalanches were numerous, with dead trees reflecting the moonlight like the bleached bones of ancient creatures that had been thrown helter-skelter down the slopes. Live trees were twisted in grotesque postures, even growing out from under boulders as they fought to survive.

As he pulled the wheel back and forth to avoid the larger rocks in his path, his headlights picked out the chaotic refuse dumped on the valley floor by forces God had set in motion eons before. It was very dark and he realized that he was too exhausted to go on. He'd had enough for one day. When the road passed under the shadows of some large trees, he braked to a stop, shut off the engine, and climbed down from the cab.

Tag-Alongs

The Bottleneck
Hidden Valley, Vermont
May 9th, 8:12 p.m.

McCord and Ross stood in the deep shadows beneath the trees on the edge of the little lake, staring at the lights of the tractor-trailer as its driver somehow got the rig around the crumbling edge of the big pond and began moving up the right side of the valley. The woman realized that she'd been unconsciously leaning to her right, willing the truck to pull clear of the lake.

"What now?" she whispered.

"One thing's certain," he replied. "We're not following that truck." There was no misinterpreting the fear in his voice. "I have little doubt that his gang is waiting up the valley for him."

He took a poncho from one of the saddle bags and wrapped it over the headlight.

"Why'd you do that?" she asked.

"Because when I start the engine, the headlamp will come on," he reminded her, the disdain evident in his reply.

She was instantly sorry that she'd asked.

In the darkness, she didn't see him shake his head in contempt. *Typical ignorant female,* he thought.

He mounted the bike, started the engine, throttled it down, and ordered her to follow on foot. Then he began riding very slowly up the left side of the lake, weaving carefully back and forth between the trees that grew between the escarpment and the lake.

He hissed at her. "Look for some place we can use as a shelter, maybe a hollow or a cave."

Paradise Found

Hidden Valley
Rt 19, Central Vermont
May 9th, 8:28 p.m.

CC stood beside the truck, gazing up at the valley walls that towered high above him on either side of the valley. Their height, and the illusion of their nearness, was accentuated by the darkness. Their looming mass would have seemed almost suffocating but for the tiny crystalline stars strewn in magnificent array across a cobalt sky.

A cricket chirped nearby, causing him to consider his own size in the scheme of things, while the stream sang a cheery counterpoint as it swept by.

He was exhausted. Climbing up on the running board, he leaned across the seat, reached into an open carton, felt for a can, and peeled off the top in the darkness. He was happily surprised to find that it contained peaches. Using the blade of his pocket knife to stab them, he ate them slowly, the aching solitude a fitting table from which to savor the sweet fruit, the hooting of an owl somewhere off in the trees adding to a sense of unreality.

Making his way to the stream bed, he knelt to rinse his hands and splash water over his face. When he returned to the truck, he crawled into the bed behind the driver's seat and fell into a troubled sleep. Images of a burning house and blanket covered victims were succeeded by those of a cursing drunk, and then a car careening across a highway toward a turgid stream.

He awoke before the birds, soaked in sweat. The cab was foul from the stale air and from his unwashed body. He'd shut the windows tightly to keep out the mosquitoes but even so, one or two had troubled him much of the night. He felt stiff and miserable.

Climbing down from the cab, a whole new world opened before him. As he rubbed the sleep from his eyes, he instantly fell in love with this strange place. The long narrow defile through which he had pulled the rig was behind him. He saw that it was merely a bottleneck that formed the hidden entrance to the canyon in which he now found himself. He was parked toward the northeastern end of the valley, the small lake just a few hundred yards behind him.

He could see now that the pond was fed by a turbulent stream that ran right up the center of the valley, more or less parallel to the narrow log road on which he'd parked. It bubbled cheerily as it swept past on his left, nearly finished with its lilting roll down the valley. Most of the canyon still lay before him, to the west. Steep rock walls stood well out to either side, with the west end of the valley shrouded in fog. The surface of the water seemed to smoke in the morning chill, but the illusion of a peaceful stream was broken as he watched an uprooted tree sweep by, then slide across the surface of the pond before coming to rest against the shore near the mouth of the conduit.

The beauty of the early morning twilight seemed pregnant with possibilities, as though the earth, brooding over the coming day, was about to burst into light and song. A blanket of fog cloaked the northwest corner of the valley. The tops of scattered evergreens pierced this gauzy river which, like the stream, seemed to flow inexorably toward him. Yet, unlike the river, the fog was not confined by earthen banks. The breeze that wafted the mist down the valley was generated by interplays of heat and cold, born of convection currents that rose from winter-chilled and solar-heated masses of rock, from icy streams, from the sun-soaked earth and from the errant solar winds born of the rising sun.

As he watched, the trees morphed from an indistinguishable black velvet to a dark mossy green, their little detail picked out with a fine brush. The matte black water of the moving stream became a churning slate gray, and the fog took on an implausible turquoise hue.

As the slopes at the far end of the valley caught the morning rays, he thought he saw a flash of light on his periphery. It came from across the lake, from the cliffside. Alarmed, he snapped his head to the left to study the pattern of shadows and light, but saw nothing unusual. He assumed that the rising sun had been reflected by a piece of mica or quartz imbedded in the northwest wall, but he nevertheless felt a vague disquiet because he was now unable to spot it.

This feeling, coupled with the sun's growing illumination of the valley, made him realize that he was dangerously exposed. The unparalleled splendor of this first morning had, for a moment, made him forget his headache and grumbling stomach, but the fear of being discovered on this open valley floor banished any thought of those small discomforts. He was overtaken by his fears of the preceding evening, and he searched the sky to see whether his airborne antagonist might have made an early start in hopes of catching a careless refugee like himself.

Again he climbed to the seat of the big cab, saddened by the realization that this might be the last time he ever moved the truck. Moreover, it might be the last motor vehicle he would ever drive. The thought sobered him. He turned the key and listened as the engine cranked, pumping the precious vaporized fuel into its hungry cylinders.

His movements were slow and deliberate. He slipped the shifting lever in and out of gear, then settled it into low. Just this one last time he wanted to feel the machinery respond to his commands for with this last drive he felt that an era was passing. He slipped the clutch, engaged it again, and finally let it completely out, feeling the torque bite the axle, the truck pulling slowly forward. He gently guided the rig up the rough, narrow wood road which lay well away from the creek that was now hidden from view by massive rock formations.

To his right, a small but beautiful series of waterfalls crashed down the canyon's north wall, then snaked across the valley floor toward the stream that bisected the valley.

Rolling forward at barely a walking pace, he swung around the larger boulders that had fallen from the canyon walls, and then had rolled hundreds of feet to lay like neglected grave markers along the overgrown roadway. When a turn in the stream's path brought it close to the road, he found that he had to get down and pry a large rock from his path so that his wide rig could move safely between the steep bank and a stone wall.

Soon he found himself among giant conifers and a grove of ancient hardwoods. He crossed through a flower-laced meadow and, as with a well-groomed woman, seemed to sense rather than smell the bouquet of its perfume. Occasionally the road

Royalty-free internet photo courtesy of John Sullivan

would cross over a narrow culvert where a foaming brook, born at the base of the cliffs on the north side of the valley, raced to unite with the larger stream on its long journey to the sea.

The stream itself was losing a little of its dynamism as he drew nearer to its source, for all down the length of the valley smaller streams had been adding their volume, resulting in the torrent that was ultimately released beneath the highway, another world away.

The big wheels of the tractor made slow but easy work of the neglected road. *Not too neglected,* he realized. Someone must have maintained the numerous culverts that carried the water beneath the road from the cliffs on his right to the stream on his left. CC was mesmerized by a herd of deer as they went leaping away across a meadow, the sun catching the white tails that seemed to wave like flags. Still the truck crept on, carrying him past the ruins of an old barn, and alongside uncultivated fields. This evidence that the valley appeared ne-glected and deserted did nothing to ease his misgivings.

The valley looked to be nearly a mile long. The trail he followed continued to parallel the right side of the stream, sometimes skirting it, sometimes drifting away into the woods and pastures, always following the easier terrain. For a time, he drove alongside a beach of hard-packed sand where weird and grotesque boulders, carved by untold centuries of wind and water, towered taller than his rig. Scoured into smooth and rounded monuments, the fantastic configurations seemed better suited to a museum of modern art than to this strange and deserted place.

He stopped the rig within a copse of tall trees where he felt reasonably safe from discovery. The air was redolent with the scent of evergreens, and he leaned back and closed his tired eyes against the glare, while he inhaled deeply to cleanse his head and heart of the shades of death which had been too long with him. He awoke in late morning, dripping with per-spiration, the sun high overhead.

It was a warm day for early May. He looked at the mas-sive rock walls that seemed to tower above him on his right, though they were actually hundreds of yards away. He real-ized that those steep cliffs would store the sun's heat as well as protect the valley from winds which would otherwise dissipate that heat. Yet the warmth brought a sense of well-being to a heart that seemed long since deadened by discouragement and death.

His clothes were filthy and clung to his sweating body. He had worked hard, and hadn't bathed in a couple of days. A bath was suddenly very important to him.

The Baptism

The "Swimming Hole"
Hidden Valley
Rt 19, Central Vermont
May 10th, Noon

CC climbed down from the truck's cab and made his way across the rock-strewn beach toward the stream.

It was wider here, and the water seemed to idle its way among the amazing boulders that rose out of its depths. The log road itself was nearly blocked from view by a number of these remarkable monoliths. Several rose nearly twenty feet above the surface of the stream, then seemed to swoop down until they disappeared into the crystal clear water which, like liquid emerald, roiled around them.

One awesome monument, rounded and smoothed by ages of flowing water, had a hole worn near its top large enough to pass a small automobile through. The huge forma-tions were like bathing dinosaurs, rising from the water, or ly-ing just beneath its surface, gray, rounded, smooth, and mas-sive.

CC stepped mincingly among the sharp stones to make his way to the stream's edge. Stripping off his filthy clothes, he dropped them on the sand. Then he stepped onto the base of what he thought of as a magnificent sculpture, and worked his way carefully up its sloped surface until he stood framed in an opening in the monolith. It was so large that he had to stretch to touch the wind-washed columns on either side. He stood there for a long moment, staring sightless across the valley, caught up with the puny insignificance of his race.

He found himself quoting aloud, "As for the days of our life, they contain seventy years, or if due to strength, eighty years..." and his voice trailed off. "...or if due to strength," he resumed, then stood stock still. He rubbed his forehead as though trying to draw out the words, persisting in the exercise because it seemed somehow important. He was surprised that he was able to complete the verse, for the words seemed to fit his mental frame like a glove.

"...Yet their pride is but labor and sorrow; For soon it is gone and we fly away."

Now, why would I have memorized that, he wondered. *The events of the past month certainly demonstrate the truth of that passage, but they don't account for my being able to recite it. Millions of people, perhaps billions, have passed into eternity in the past month, and when winter comes, and what little food that remains is consumed, millions more will perish.*

He examined the massive monoliths that rose all around him. It was obvious that they had once formed the shell of the earth, but over the centuries water had cut deep into the earth's crust, scouring out the softer stone, leaving these remarkable monuments behind.

For eons, they have stood stubbornly against the forces of nature, and they will be standing long after I am dust, he thought. *They have been continually attacked by water, wind, earth, and ice, but change had been slow. It's as though they were carved by the finger of God.*

He thought about what he'd quoted. *"And yet our pride,"* he paraphrased, *"is but labor and sorrow."* It led him to compare his present paltry existence with these ageless monoliths which wouldn't see a hundredth of their bulk worn away in the brief period of his entire lifetime. And in all this natural splendor he was reminded of the First Cause of all that existed. It was as though God had placed them in this place just to point out his temporal state, and to remind him that the only way to eternal life was through faith in Him.

I might possibly survive for three-score years and ten, he mused, *but how I live out my days or years is far more important than the number of years I'm given.*

CC studied the surface of the monoliths carefully, and moved to an area where the rock formed a natural slide that disappeared far below the surface of the crystal clear water. He sat down and let himself go. Moving at a breathtaking rate he plunged deep beneath the surface. Though it was a warm spring day, the icy water of the mountain stream seemed to tear the breath from him and he gasped with the shock of it. He splashed his way toward the surface by chasing the sun's rays. It took a few quick strokes to return to the rock and pull himself up onto the ledge. The drops that he shook from his arms shone in the sunlight like diamonds.

Cold, yes, but he felt a tremendous exhilaration, and so he dove deep into the pool, daring it to sweep him away, to consume him in its grip. It did neither, and adjusting to the cold he swam slowly beneath the surface, sweeping his arms in a slow breast stroke, nurturing his air, and gazing through the clear water at the incredible shapes around him. Then with three hard strokes he swept to the surface where he drew in a deep breath before letting out a whoop of joy.

Again, he pulled himself from the rolling stream and, shivering with the cold, stepped back upon the shore where he reclaimed his shoes and dirty clothing, bundling them in his arms. He moved carefully across the shallows where the softer rock had been scoured away, stepping warily around one dark and forbidding pot hole that was so deep that he couldn't see its bottom.

He found another pothole in the shape of a large bathtub. It was filled with sun-warmed water, and was continually washed and replenished by a rivulet which flowed in on the upstream side, and emptied through a small crack at the downstream end.

Photo by Frank Becker, ©2014, all rights reserved.

CC set his shoes on a dry rock, then stepped carefully down into the pool, clothes and all. It came to his knees, and it was as satisfying as a whirlpool bath. Piece by piece, he pounded the garments gently with a round stone, just as primitive peoples had washed their clothes through the ages. Then he let them swirl about him, to be rinsed by the streams unceasing action. He let them soak for a while, then wrung them all out and spread them over nearby rocks to dry in the rising heat.

When he had completed washing his clothes, he lowered himself carefully into the pool, lay back, and let it work the aches and stress from his body. He let his mind go completely blank for a while, just lying there, the water moving slowly around his weary body. He relaxed so completely that all that existed seemed to be his essence, floating in a sea of serenity.

Catharsis

The "Swimming Hole"
Hidden Valley west of State Road 19
Central Vermont
May 10th, 1:22 p.m.

After a time his body began to signal that it was surfeited. He'd lost the sense of pleasure, and was beginning to feel slightly uncomfortable. He'd had enough. His mind returned involuntarily to his present crisis.

Rising from the pool, a breeze, a mere zephyr, chilled him. He stood naked, a marble statue in a sculpture garden, the animate man surveying the spectacular size and beauty of the inanimate statuary surrounding him.

He began to weep quietly, then to choke and sob uncontrollably. Was he going mad? Had he finally collapsed under the pressures he'd been experiencing for the past month? What about his ability to spout a Bible verse? Was that some indication of his identity? *It has to be,* he thought, *but I don't want to think about that right now.* In anguish he shouted aloud, "I just can't!" He was shocked at his outcry, then realized that he was simply overwhelmed.

He didn't know who he was. He didn't know his name, nor what he had done with his life, much less whom he might have hurt or helped. He felt an awful sense of loss, and he cried out unexpectedly, "Lord Jesus, please help me!" It was neither a question nor a command. It was a vehement plea, a powerful prayer which was so simple and elemental in its composition that it encompassed his world and his entire lifetime. He'd seen so much horror in the past month that issues of life seemed cut and dried. He choked out the words, "Lord, I do not know my past, but I promise you — no matter what I face — I will try to make my future count." His sobbing abruptly ceased. He took a deep breath, and felt a remarkable sense of peace flood his being.

This was catharsis. This was the cleansing of his emotions. More, this was the purgation of his soul. He'd made his confession and his commitment, though in the short conscious lifetime since he'd awakened as an amnesiac in an X-ray room, he could think of little enough for which he must confess.

Nevertheless, he'd had his bath, his baptism. Somehow, all the unknown pain, the fear, the horrible experience of the past few weeks — even the secret memories lost to his amnesia — none of it mattered any longer. The past, like the world that might exploit it, was dead. And he sensed that, whatever he might have done, he was forgiven. He felt like a new man, born unto a new beginning, and he was determined to make the most of it.

At some time, during that cleansing bath, he had concluded that the discovery of this valley, with all of its remarkable twists and turns, presaged a new life. It seemed odd that much of the world was in the midst of a self-made catastrophe, and yet he had come to view his situation almost as an opportunity. To him this realization represented a spiritual epiphany as well as life-saving discovery.

Raising his face to the azure sky, a tumultuous shout of joy burst from his lips. He stood with arms spread toward the heavens in an uninhibited display of thanksgiving and dedicated his new life to the unseen God who had brought him safe to this haven.

"Well, I'll Be..."

"Hidden Valley"
Central Vermont
May 10th, 12:40 p.m.

McCord was kneeling on the ledge at the mouth of the cave, staring out across the valley. As he swept his eyes the length of the stream, he suddenly took in a breath and whispered, "Well, I'll be!"

"What do you see," she demanded.

"Uh," he temporized, forcing a laugh, "the guy parked the truck under the trees over there."

It's not possible! he thought. *I'm too far away to be sure, but it just can't be! Everything was so well-planned. He couldn't have survived. And how would he have come upon this particular hiding place? What luck!*

The woman's voice intruded on his musings "Where?" she demanded peremptorily.

"Huh? Where, what?"

"Where did he park the truck?"

He hesitated, then pointed across the valley. "See where the log road passes that copse of hardwoods beyond the stream?"

"Jim," she responded irritably, "the stream goes the entire length of the valley."

"Over there, where those huge boulders look like they're growing out of the water."

"Oh, yes, I see the trees."

"Do you see it? The truck is parked under the trees."

"Ah, I see the truck," she laughed. "I wonder where he is," and she began scanning the area between the truck and the stream. "Oh, there he is, down by the water." Then she gasped. "I don't think he's wearing anything!"

A moment before, McCord had been admiring the man as he saw him standing atop a gigantic boulder, his hands raised to the sky, but he was surprised at her reaction, and turned to look at her. Her face was rose colored. She was clearly embarrassed.

And this is the tough, worldly woman we all heard about on the news! he thought, and opened his mouth to mock her. Then he had a thought: *Her innocence may be something I can make use of later on.*

Another Discovery

"Hidden Valley"

Central Vermont

May 10th, 2:40 p.m.

Unaware that he had an audience, CC began gathering up his clothing. Each garment had that slightly stiff, wind-blown, sun-warmed smell that provides a feeling of luxury and well-being, and each item added an additional layer of well-being as he pulled it on.

Climbing back up into the cab of the truck, he again moved it forward. He had nearly reached the northwest corner of the canyon when he stopped once more to survey the general area which he hoped would serve as his new home. Ahead on the right stood a thick growth of mature evergreens, and rising behind them, between the pines and the cliffs, he could make out the crowns of many huge old hard-woods, their leaves just beginning to open.

Guiding the truck forward, he pulled beneath the forest's spreading canopy, again taking care to hide the rig from aerial observation. For the moment, his situation seemed too good to be true. He realized that he was world-weary, hungering for the security that only privacy — or the illusion of privacy — might offer. He wanted to be left alone, to allow time for things to work themselves out. Above all, he needed to avoid confrontation. He still suffered from frequent headaches, and his days and dreams remained troubled.

Under these circumstances, who wouldn't be troubled? With few exceptions, those who have survived this long will have to continue to struggle to survive the war's aftermath — and that will prove a continual long-term challenge. War is a great leveler, he thought, *not just of cities, but of social orders and petty posturings. Rich or poor will find that most of the formerly comfortable population centers are death-traps. The cities will be tainted by famine, disease, and brutality, ostensibly caused by nuclear radiation, but primarily because of man's inhumanity to man. Most survivors will have had to leave their homes, and when they became refugees, they will be subject to every imaginable indignity. The worst enemy of man remains unregenerate man, coldly self-centered, and often the unwitting tool of the devil.*

Because it was dangerous to be near other human be-ings, CC had sought after and discovered the undiscoverable. He had stumbled upon a mountain hideaway that appeared to be virtually unknown to the outside world. Perhaps stum-bled was not the right word. CC might not know his own identity, but he was coming to believe that he knew, and was known by, someone far greater.

Phrases were dancing through his mind, thoughts like, "...all things work together for good to those that love God...." CC did not know why he could quote that particular Bible verse either, but he knew that he would be unthankful if he did not acknowledge the God who had led him to this poten-tial home.

Yet he could not shake his vague sense of disquiet. He was like a dog worrying at a decayed bone. The more he gnawed at it, the less satisfying he found it. Why, he wondered, hadn't this marvelous hiding place become the summer home of some millionaire? Barring that, why wasn't it listed on maps as a state or national park? Instead there was only that weather-beaten old sign — "Hidden Valley." Yet, considering the timing involved in his making this discovery, he considered it the richest gift he had ever received. At the same time, he couldn't help but conclude that since he had stumbled upon this valley, others would ultimately discover it too.

CC appreciated the fact that his situation was extraordinary. While a dwindling population was being forced into small designated holding areas and concentration camps, he appeared to have dominion over an entire valley of his own. Since it seemed unlikely that any but government officials and the military would be doing much traveling, the likelihood of his valley being discovered was small. Hunters might be a danger, but since the government was discouraging ownership of firearms, they too seemed of little concern.

He had not yet discovered anything here that would be of interest to others, neither crops nor animals. So there seemed to be little likelihood that someone would intentionally seek this place. With things going as well as they had been, he might be forgiven a bit of overconfidence, but he was anything but that.

He was increasingly concerned with his mood swings, and found himself compensating for any sudden euphoria by remaining braced for the unexpected. Yet the constant strain that was revealed by the grooves around his mouth were too deep to have been formed in just the past month. He assumed they were the result of past battles and unremembered difficulties. Still, In spite of everything he couldn't help feeling a little upbeat.

And though his mind seemed to be counseling prudence, he had begun to recognize within himself a spirit that would occasionally take a dare. In the current situation, there was little point in holding back. To stand still would be to die.

I have to be willing to take risks. If I don't locate a place to settle down very soon, I'll either be captured by unknown enemies or overcome by my environment.

His behavior over the past few weeks had caused him to conclude that he was a proactive kind of person. His behavior indicated that he preferred to head off and prevent problems rather than later find himself faced with the dilemma of solving them. On the other hand, there also appeared to be something in him which preferred the challenge of a crisis to the discipline of preparedness.

He couldn't know whether he had been wounded by such forays in the past, if indeed there were any such, but right now he found himself relishing the possibility of facing and conquering the unknown and the unexpected. It was something he sensed about himself rather than something that was knowable. Maybe it was the fact that his life could end any moment that gave him a sense of living on the edge, a sort of "I don't give a darn" attitude. Time would tell.

Am I mentally unstable? he wondered. And am I a different person from the man I was before my head injury? If so, perhaps it's because I'm not restrained by memory, conscience or law. When I was in the hospital, I discovered that I didn't like making lists and estimating my needs, but I stuck to it. Yet I know that I'm not detail-oriented, not a bean counter. Does that make me irresponsible?

The last time he'd looked in a mirror, he'd noticed laugh lines about his gray eyes. *Those,* he had thought, *belie a general bitterness.* At the same time, he knew that a cynicism had grown within him, and any astute observer would recognize him to be both an intense and confused man. Yet, he recognized it as a healthy sign that even now he frequently laughed at himself.

He snorted aloud. There were simply too many unanswered questions about his past, as well as his own mental stability, for him to feel any enduring peace. It really didn't matter. He didn't have the luxury to worry about it. He shook his head angrily as he sought to clear the dark clouds away and get back to far more urgent business – survival.

Standing beneath the trees at the edge of the glade, he looked across the valley. Strange, he thought. When he'd been at the lower end of the valley, it had looked fairly level, but as he looked down its length, he was surprised at how far he'd driven uphill. Although the eye might not detect changes in elevation, the stream's numerous small waterfalls and plunging cataracts made it obvious that there was a dramatic difference in elevation.

He could now see that the valley was shaped like a long-necked bottle laid on its side. The narrow opening through which he'd entered pointed east. The valley was almost three-eighths of a mile wide. Apart from the narrow bottleneck through which he'd entered, it maintained that approximate width from end to end. From its western base to the bottleneck, was over three quarters of a mile.

Paradise Lost

Northwest Corner of Hidden Valley
May 11th, 2:17 p.m.

He climbed back into the cab, and continued along the old log road that now wound beneath the trees until he'd reached the extreme northwest corner of the valley. Satisfied that the rig was still well hidden from any passing aircraft, he climbed down and began trudging toward the cliffs.

The land here was idyllic. The tree trunks were like great columns, their canopies spreading out and intertwining high above. Without leaves, they were like the stone tracery supporting the ceiling of a great cathedral, the limbs seemed to frame and support the turquoise sky suspended above them.

Beneath his feet, however, the ground was thickly mulched with leaves and moss.

He wandered onto a small meadow that lay between the forest and the cliff. Trillium and myrtle added bright spots of color to the carpet of spring grass that spread from the wood in which he'd parked the truck, to the fallen boulders that lay beneath the cliff walls. Moss and lichen clung stubbornly to those pale walls that soared high above him, forming fantastic tapestries.

Here and there mounds of rubble were ringed with saplings and scrubby growth that had somehow caught hold and grown among the broken rock. Huge slabs lay tossed here and there, cluttering the area, reminding him of the cairns of long dead kings. His mind wandered off in search of where he might have been exposed to a word like "cairns." Oddly, he could feel a cold draft, as though the ghosts of those dead kings were breathing on him, and he didn't know whether he shivered from actual cold or in unexpected superstition.

He was not insensitive to the dreamlike beauty of the place, and fought consciously to rivet his attention on the possible dangers and potential benefits. Natural beauty was pleasant, but definitely not essential to his survival.

He made his way toward some gnarled trees whose ancient roots twisted and turned in odd patterns over and around the boulders, making it appear as though they were climbing the cliff. Their growth gave the illusion of men spreadeagled on the rock face, their lives hanging by their toes and fingertips. Beneath their branches grew a tangle of sumac trees, their berries punctuating the green leaves with blotches of red brown.

This wild melange was interwoven with the thick vines of the wild grape, just now breaking into its profusion of spring growth, lush with new leaves. The cliff was striated here, and it appeared as though great stone roots reached out into the valley floor.

Here and there the huge rock surface upon which the lush meadow grass clung had been split by unknown forces, creating long, narrow cracks, like stone trenches that criss-crossed one another. They were each deep and wide enough for men to walk along them in single file and not have their head show above the surface. CC stepped carefully to avoid falling into them.

As he moved toward the cliffs, he found himself among the tangle of trees and sumac that grew in their shadows. He recognized other old and neglected trees. There were apple, pear, and cherry trees, now almost overgrown by sumac and wild grape. Looking about on the ground for any rotting fruit that would indicate they were still productive, a slight movement caught his eye.

He felt a weird sensation, and realized that the hair on his arms was actually standing up. He had walked into a nest of timber rattlers. Several were coiled and within striking distance. Without seeming to give it any thought, and just as one struck, he leapt for a limb that was just above shoulder height. The snake's fangs sank into the heel of his shoe, and as he struggled to pull himself up and over the limb, the serpent dropped away.

CC's breathing became coarse and ragged, and an icy chill shook his body. He was almost rigid with fear, but it was something more than the fear of death. He fought desperately to break the hold of the terror that gripped him. He could smell the peculiar reek of the snakes now, along with the pungent odor of crushed mint. A mockingbird sang nearby, its lilting song creating an odd counterpoint to the insidious rasping of the snake's scales as they slithered below him.

Another rattler struck for his leg, but came up short, recoiling itself instantly as it fell back to the ground. These reptiles were aroused, and he was justifiably frightened. He had an image of himself lying there among them, puncture marks discoloring his flesh, fangs striking him again and again, his eyes opened sightless to the sky.

An overactive imagination isn't doing much for my confidence, he concluded.

The branch over which he lay was about eight inches thick. He twisted his torso as he tried to pull himself up to lay on it, but his shirt was dragged loose from his trousers, and the rough bark tore at his stomach. He wanted to slide back-ward, to escape the barbed-like bark, but he instead opted to pull himself further up the limb, preferring the relatively pure wounds made by the bark to those the snakes would produce. In fact, he only resented the difficulty he had in dragging him-self further into its arms and away from the snakes below.

He reached for a smaller limb just above his head. Then, kneeling awkwardly on the lower limb, he rose carefully to his feet. Though he was momentarily safe, icy sweat covered his body and his stomach had become a knot of anxiety. He looked down and began counting the serpents, but lost track when he reached a dozen. They must have been resting there in the cool dampness, avoiding the mid-day heat of the nearby sun-drenched rocks. Their blind eyes all seemed to stare intently in his direction, and he was convulsed with an involuntary spasm of fear and disgust. He hated snakes.

There was suddenly a sea shift in his thinking. *This valley is not really paradise. What's that line from the Bible? Something about the judgment of God on the race following Adam's fall — thorns, sick-ness, death, oh, and labor by the sweat of one's brow. Kind of a collec-tive catch-all for all the maladies facing the race since man's disgraceful fall in the Garden.*

"Add snakes," he groaned aloud, almost regaining his sense of humor.

Serpents should be first! he thought. *It all started with that ser-pent's temptation. Or did it start with the serpent realizing that man was susceptible to his temptations? Doesn't make much difference. These snakes tempted me to doubt the care of an all-loving God. They also rep-resent the very real possibility that I'll meet up with that God sooner than I had hoped. A trial, a temptation? Absolutely. But the bottom line is that I'm still alive!*

His dilemma brought him back to cold reality. Natural and man-made forces could work either in his favor or against him, here as well as anywhere, and he would have to quickly learn to coexist or he would perish. If he were injured, he would be alone, with only the help of God to minister healing to him. Even a minor disability, such as a single snake bite, could result in untimely death. And the very real and immediate possibility that he might suffer the bites of numerous rattlesnakes did little to improve his outlook.

His fingers ached, and he realized he was squeezing the limb above him in a death grip, afraid both to move and afraid to remain still. He forced himself to breathe evenly, trying to relax each muscle in his body, assuring himself that everything would be all right, that anyone would have cause to become somewhat irrational in a situation like this.

He tried to laugh again in order to relieve the tension, but all that came out was a pathetic parody, a near-hysterical giggle. The sound made him laugh again — this time at the futility of trying to appear poised and blasé in a life-threatening situation — especially when his only audience was the nest of vipers.

He looked down the length of the nearly horizontal limb of the gnarled old tree and saw that it crossed the limb of another. Grapevines nearly as thick as his wrists hung between the trees, rooting themselves down among their trunks and climbing upward until they disappeared in the shadows of the cliff above. It occurred to him that he might use them to bear some of his weight as he tried to make his way from tree to tree away from the serpent's nesting place.

He couldn't see very far through the dense branches, but anyplace else seemed a far better location than this. Visibility and movement were impaired by the confusion of the lush growth. The entire area around him was a tangle of branches and vines. Fear had made his shoulders and neck painfully stiff, and he could scarcely force his body to respond. He fought to relax.

He almost lost his grip when he thought he heard a voice say, "This sort of lifestyle could kill a guy." He was startled until he realized it was he that had spoken. A harsh uncertain bellow, a Teddy Roosevelt guffaw, burst from him, then he suddenly found himself laughing hysterically, inanely, stupidly.

The racket he was making was met by the rustling movements of the half-score of snakes immediately below him, each defying him to leave his perch and face their wrath. Abruptly he choked off his giggling. He moved on, but with little confidence. He realized that he had providentially found himself nestled in a hardwood, for if he had grabbed the limb of one of the treacherous sumacs, it would have broken under his weight and left him lying among the snakes.

What momentarily sobered him was the fact that this was not the first time he'd caught himself talking to himself. During his first few days in the hospital, he'd found himself speaking aloud. Initially, he had wondered whether he was going insane. Subsequent strange behavior almost convinced him that he was. Then he'd remembered someone joking that, "It's okay to talk to yourself, but you should become concerned if you start answering back." On another occasion, he'd read that people who talk to themselves are often of higher intelligence. *Great rationale,* he thought. Nevertheless, he couldn't shake the fear that he was not entirely sane.

Then he reasoned, *Why shouldn't I talk to myself? Since I don't have anyone else to talk with, no one to test my thoughts or to share ideas, this might serve as a useful mental mechanism. And if carrying on a conversation with myself sobers me, and makes me weigh my actions more carefully, it might not be such a bad thing.*

Then he admitted that he was probably kidding himself. He concluded that he was losing control and was at best neurotic. *I'm over-thinking everything,* he thought. After grappling with these concerns for a time, he had concluded that he was increasingly troubled because he had no one else, no human companion, with whom he could share his feelings or discuss his ideas.

So he sublimated by attempting to turn his questionable behavior into a healing dialogue. At first, he had been very hesitant to enter into this practice. *When someone starts talking to invisible people,* he thought, *he is generally thought to be insane. And if I started hearing someone answering back, I suppose I'd be so far around that bend that I'd no longer even realize it.*

At that point, he tried to square his reasoning with what he thought he knew of the Bible.

I wouldn't be talking to myself, or to some alter ego, if I were addressing God. The Bible not only states that I can talk to God, but that I should talk to him.

He had pondered the concept of prayer for a day or so. Not community prayer, but individual, isolated prayer — just between himself and God.

He began to pretend that God was a close friend, one who was intimately and immediately concerned with every aspect of his life. Inasmuch as Christians are taught that God is both omnipresent and omniscient — that is, that everyone is always immediately in His presence, and that God knows everything about everything, this idea offered him surprising comfort. God would be his mentor!

Then he began to feel foolish because this great epiphany of his was simply the conclusion that every Christian was supposed to reach. The believer, after all, is to pray without ceasing, and certainly this sort of dialogue was precisely what that command meant. So, instead of talking to himself, or casting his words out into an indifferent universe, he was chatting with the One who sticks closer than a brother.

I will not be reaching out to some non-entity, some figment of my imagination, or some artificial substitute for a companion, like a statue or a volleyball, he thought. *Something like that would be a mark of insanity, or worse, idol worship. In my case, I'm speaking to the living God.*

CC remembered how he had gotten a Bible out and had begun studying passages dealing with prayer.

I might, for example, ask the Lord, "What do you think of this plan?" And, I might, but almost certainly wouldn't, hear an audible re-

ply. If I'm quiet and attentive for a sufficient period, I might "hear" a still small voice say something like, "This is the way; walk ye in it." Or God might somehow nudge me in the right direction by bringing to mind some heretofore forgotten concept."

It's even conceivable that He might ask me a question, like, "What do you have in mind, CC?" Or, "I'm sure you can think of a better alternative, CC." Or some new idea might inexplicably flash across my mind. And God, might even offer alternatives, or specific instructions. Or allow me to walk into a wall, or through a heretofore invisible door.

One thing seems clear, he thought. *I won't be dealing with an alter ego. I'm won't be partitioning my mind, or creating a separate character in my subconscious. I won't be a split personality. Or calling up a familiar spirit, or practicing divination or witchcraft. My kindred spirit will not simply serve as a sounding board off which I will bounce my ideas, or serve as some sort of a devil's advocate. And, unlike the New Age crowd, I won't be speaking to a demon, or be guided by the devil himself.*

He'd grimaced at the implication. *No. God is anything but the Devil's advocate. God is God! Satan is a fallen angel. Anyway, no matter how I refer to him, God is far more than a figment of my imagination. He is the Creator who sustains me and helps keep me on the straight and narrow. His is not a voice out of my own subconscious, but a voice from heaven, helping me question my motives and my decisions, and thereby steadying me when I'm in danger of doing something impulsive or self-destructive. He's not simply eternal, He's internal...* "Christ in you, the hope of glory!"

CC thought back to a month earlier, and imagined that he could see the nuclear missiles diving through the clouds, with entire cities disappearing forever. He placed the palm of one hand on his forehead, as though to dispel the image and the pain it caused.

When he opened his eyes, he again found himself teetering on the forgotten limb, still grasping the branch above. His concern about his sanity had vanished when he'd remembered that the thoughts of his alter ego really weren't his own subconscious thoughts at all, but were those of the One whose wisdom and experience infinitely exceeded his own. He considered it a matter of faith, but God had confirmed His love through empirical evidence, things that he could see, touch, taste, hear and smell. The wonderful things he had experienced, the things that had resulted in his survival, had been beyond the scope of his own imagination, intelligence, and understanding.

That's why a valid prayer relationship is ultimately pragmatic, he realized. *It bears fruit. Though we may not see immediate evidence, or may misinterpret what we're seeing, God is faithful.*

He wondered whether he'd ever felt this close to God prior to this catastrophe, before the loss of his memory. Then he realized that we tend to ignore God until we face a crisis. Whatever the explanation, it didn't matter. He would simply revel in a relationship which most people could never even imagine.

An Uneasy Peace

Southeast corner, "Hidden Valley"
May 11th, 2:35 p.m.

McCord snarled at Ross. "I told you to start gathering tree branches to make a lean-to over against that cliff face."

"And I told you that there is a hillside of broken rock above that cliff face that could come crashing down on us at any moment," she retorted.

"Frankly, I'm not much interested in your opinions. If you plan to stay with me, you'll do what I say, and you'll do it the moment I say it!"

"And, frankly, I have no intention of blindly following a stranger whose knowledge, at least under these circumstances, is far inferior to my own."

"Well," he replied, maybe it's time for you to move on."

"Precisely what I was thinking," she shot back. She picked up her belongings and, without a word, turned and started up the valley. After about fifty yards, she started to climb the cliff. His eyes followed her as she climbed to a ledge about twenty feet above the valley floor, and made as to enter a narrow cave.

"All right, we'll go there," he shouted after her.

"I didn't invite you to join me."

"So what!" he answered, and began pushing his motorcycle over the rock strewn terrain toward her.

Shrugging her shoulders in frustration, she sat down on a rock to wait for him. She thought she heard something padding about inside the cave, and with a grin she decided to let him enter first so that he could claim the discovery.

A Serpent in the Garden

Northwest Corner of Hidden Valley
May 11th, 3:10 p.m.

CC could now see the cliff through the branches. The limb upon which he stood had grown against the stubborn stone of the near vertical wall.

Pressing itself against a rocky ledge, the limb had bent upward, its heliotropic hunger satisfied only by the exposure of its leaves to the warm caress of the sun that bathed the stony shelf that barred its path. Its bark had been scored by constant rubbing against the stone, but its flowing sap had bandaged the wound, and the limb was little weakened by its mindless assault on the stone shelf.

The cliff, too, had suffered wear, but it did not fare as well, for while the tree had repaired itself, the cliff could not. A millennia of weathering had created numerous fissures in the rock, and the slow growing limb had continued the work, scraping the fractures until some of the detritus had broken free, the stones falling to the ground below, leaving a natural gutter in the edge of the shelf through which rain water poured from the ledge to the ground below. The process of disintegration accelerated. Over the years, the flowing water and expanding ice had enlarged that shallow trough.

CC peered up toward the ledge and concluded that he could reach its safety from the limb on which he stood. This seemed the best place, the only place, to make the move from limb to cliff in order to escape the snakes below. Slightly off balance, he leaned forward, released his grip on the limb above him, reached out to cup both hands over the edge of the rock shelf that was just above his head, and placed his right foot on a smaller branch that protruded upward from the limb on which he stood.

His weight was now evenly distributed between his legs and arms, and he could feel himself at that precise balance point where he must risk all and thrust himself up onto the ledge, or drop back down to the limb, risking a misstep that might find him crashing to the ground below. He steeled himself for the leap, hoping to grasp some unseen protrusion or crack in the ledge, so that he could pull his upper body up into the trough.

Might as well get it over with, he thought. He took a deep breath, stiffened his arms, and pulled himself up. At the same instant he leapt up from the smaller limb, hoping that it would not twist or break beneath his weight. Springing upward, he pulled his head and shoulders up and over the surface of the ledge.

As he jumped, he realized that he hadn't bothered holding one of his little conversations with the Lord that he'd been making so much of just a few minutes earlier. While in the midst of that disquieting realization, he shifted his eyes from his feet to focus on the shelf, only to realize that the handy root or rock he'd hoped to grab hold of didn't exist. Instead he found himself staring into the eyes of another rattler, this one lying in the shade of the trough into which his chest and arms were about to drop.

The snake had a hypnotic effect on him, and his overactive imagination again took hold. As fear pumped additional adrenaline through his system, events seemed to move in slow motion. His entire being concentrated on the open mouth of the serpent. It was so close that he imagined he could dive down its distended maw. Even in motion, he seemed to hang there suspended between sky and earth, or more aptly, heaven and hell.

He was no longer conscious of time or space, but he could hear, as though amplified, the horrifying rattling of the scales as the snake, with impossible speed, drew its length into a coil. He found himself fascinated by the fact that the serpent's head did not seem to move at all, but hung suspended a few inches above the rock while it rapidly wound its body round and round beneath it to coil itself in preparation for its strike. Its blind eyes seemed locked on his. It seemed to probe his soul, holding him spellbound with fear, almost in a state of suspended animation. But he wasn't imagining the gaping mouth, distended nostrils, blind slanting eyes, and extended fangs dripping toxin?

CC's entire universe became a mere shadowed penumbra surrounding scaly death. His mouth was rigid with the rictus of fear. Craving oblivion, he wanted to will himself away from there, but he was caught in flight, a ballistic missile catapulted upward by his own arms and legs. There was no time for decision, no possible action he could imagine. One of his feet struck a protruding limb just as his chest struck the ledge, causing his body to slip to the side. At the same instant, he slapped his hands against the face of the cliff in childlike denial, and the jarring impact resulted in his falling backward and sideways. The snake struck just as he began his fall, uncoiling its mass in one fluid motion that defied focus, its assault aimed unerringly at his face.

He felt a stunning blow to his cheek as the serpent went sailing out past him, both he and the snake tumbling away from the cliff together, their weight and thrust carrying them out and down an arm's length apart.

Everything continued moving far too fast for comprehension. CC's foot caught on a limb and tipped him further sideways. His arms windmilled wildly as he began a backward plunge. He became entangled in limbs and vines, his body twisting and tearing in their grip. No time to imagine that he had survived a nuclear war only to die of snakebite or a crushing fall, or that he would end his life alone and unremembered, broken across a boulder a score of feet below, or poisoned by the nest of vipers. Without thinking, he whispered, "Please Lord!"

He rolled and tumbled as the screen of vines and branches slowed his fall. "Praise God," he whispered, caring nothing for the pain as, scraping and burning, he felt the speed of his fall arrested. He tensed in anticipation of the impact, but instead experienced a jarring pain to his upper back as his fall was abruptly interrupted, his mouth snapping shut, the breath hammered from his lungs.

The Cavern

Northwest Corner of Hidden Valley

May 11th, 3:35 p.m.

The pain was so severe that he almost lost consciousness. He'd had the wind knocked out of him, and was starved for oxygen, but when he tried to inhale, the knifelike pain in his chest was excruciating. He dare not move.

After a moment, he tried to focus on his situation. He was lying face up, his right leg tangled in a vine about six feet above the ground. A larger vine was beneath his back, a foot or so lower, and it was causing severe pain. He had probably torn the vine loose, and it had fallen with him, dragging through the branches enough to bear his weight and save his life, but at the same time, it evidently cracked one or more of his ribs. The rattler that had struck at him was writhing a few feet above his chest, mouth agape, impaled on the broken point of a dead branch.

CC wanted to move, to get away, but he was afraid he might have broken his own back in the fall. The snake's head slipped a few inches closer, and CC tried to jerk his body away, but was stopped short by the sharp pain in his side. The snake, unable to free itself from the branch, slowed its struggles and finally hung there motionless. He watched, mesmerized, as a drop of fluid formed on the tip of one of its fangs, then slowly slipped free, dropping to splash on the front of CC's shirt.

He ignored the pain in his back as he grasped a low hanging limb and pulled frantically in order to slide his body out from under the snake, and the large vine on which he was laying moving slightly with him. "No snake kabob for me, thank you," he gasped. He rolled onto his side, moving very carefully to prevent jarring his ribs further. Leaning forward, he placed his feet on the ground and slowly pulled himself erect.

He realized that he had to get away from the nest of snakes which was only a few yards away. He was staggering toward the cliff, his hand pressed against his chest in a vain effort to contain the pain, well away from the huge slabs of rock under which more snakes might be nesting. He looked up, wondering whether he had the wherewithal to again drag himself up into a tree, when he felt a chill and musty draft.

Peering through the thick foliage that shrouded the cliff on his right, he found himself staring through the foliage into the dark mouth of a cave. He stood there, twisted with pain, straining his eyes to penetrate the darkness. He couldn't decide whether he was willing to enter the cave. His mind was muddled by the shock of the fall, the persistent pain, the proximity of death, and this new revelation.

It was a moment before he realized that his only alternatives were climbing the cliff or going back through the rattlesnake's lair. Neither seemed acceptable. On the other hand, he had to ask himself what dangers he might face in the cave and whether he was likely to find another exit? Was he in fact likely to find his way out at all?

A snake, slithering toward him, decided the issue, and the possibilities inherent in the discovery of the cave tipped the scale. So much so, in fact, that he would not allow himself to be hindered. Except for one thing.

He bowed his head and closed his eyes. "Thank you, Lord, for saving my life...again." He looked around, then bowed his head again. "I don't know what to do, Lord." And since he was between the devil and the deep blue sea, or more aptly, between the rattlesnakes and the earth's maw, he felt he wasn't going to receive any better instruction. So he opted for the unknown, and pushed his way through the tangle of vines to enter the mouth of the cave.

Turning to look back, CC noted that the same vast network of vines and creepers that had served to break his fall would, even in winter, hide this cave from prying eyes. And, in summer, few casual explorers would care to challenge the rattlers to reach this small corner of the valley. What's more, the heaps of rock here and there would discourage most hikers from coming too near. Those piles of rock, which he'd romanticized as the burial mounds of long-dead kings, were evidently tailings — heaps of broken earth left behind as the refuse of some long-forgotten mining operation.

Through receding waves of pain, he forced his mind to work. He had read somewhere that satellites, hundreds of miles above the earth, once photographed its surface many times each day. They had monitored weather conditions, probed military secrets, surveyed agricultural production, and noted transportation patterns. He had once seen a photograph, purportedly taken from ten miles up, that showed a man standing on the steps of the U.S. Capitol on a cloudy day. Infra-red cameras with sophisticated lenses and computer enhanced imagery could pin-point and identify a target in total darkness, simply from the heat radiated by the human body.

With advances in computer technology, the United States and other countries, particularly China, had produced enormous fleets of drones, unmanned flying machines of every size and description. These devices served as spies in the sky as well as deadly attack vehicles. They were nearly undetectable and almost impossible to combat, especially in any number. One could be overhead right now, photographing his movements, and he wouldn't even know it. If any of these drones had survived the war, they posed an immediate threat. He needed a place to remain undetected.

If the size of this tunnel was any indication, this cave might be large enough to meet his needs. The entrance was easily fourteen feet wide and as many feet high. It would provide him with a natural fallout shelter and would safeguard him from potential exposure to sophisticated devices, whether satellites or unmanned drones.

He remembered reading somewhere that most caves maintain a steady 52-degree temperature throughout the year, assuring him a shelter in which he could survive the bitterest weather. He'd have to find a way to overcome the dampness and the gloom, and perhaps he was being premature in his judgment, but he was exulting in what he saw as God's provision of a relatively warm and secure home.

As he examined the cave, he was surprised that he could see light further in. He walked about thirty yards inward, and discovered a fork in the tunnel. Instead of walking further into the cave, he turned left and followed this man-made tunnel back toward daylight. There were no vines hanging over this second portal. He looked around carefully before stepping out onto the edge of the meadow. Looking to his left about fifty yards, he saw the vines that covered the mouth of the other tunnel, and beyond that the grove of trees where the snakes made their home.

He'd had enough of war's desolation for one day. His chest hurt, he was hungry, and he needed to rest. *Tomorrow will be soon enough to explore this cave,* he thought. He moved out across the meadow and into the woods, not surprised to discover that he'd exited the mountain close to where he'd parked the tractor-trailer.

In for a Penny...

Early exploration
Northwest Corner of Hidden Valley
May 12th, 8:55 a.m.

CC forced himself to remain in bed far later than usual. He wanted to take advantage of a couple of extra hours to rest and give his injuries time to heal.

Finally he rose, heated an MRE for breakfast, then made his way back towards the two cave portals he'd discovered the day before, carrying a stout stick in his hand against the possibility of meeting another rattlesnake.

As he walked toward the clearing that lay before the caves, his mind was elsewhere.

The commercial imitation of the military packaged meal is palatable, he thought ruefully, but nothing to write home about, if I indeed have a home. What's worse, those meals are probably as good as I may expect for a long, long time.

Reaching the opening in the cliff wall furthest from the rattlesnakes' nesting place, he twisted the vines together so that more light would enter.

They look like giant window curtains, he thought, just before he entered the cave. In spite of his labors, the additional light penetrated only a short distance into the cave.

Feeling the hair rise on the back of his neck, he turned to discover a rattler, still some distance away, zigzagging in his direction. Grimacing with the pain from his cracked rib, he threw a rock, and the snake turned away. Stopping to allow a moment for his eyes to adjust to the gloom, he pulled a flash-light from his pocket and aimed it up the tunnel. As he started up the slope of smooth limestone, he found it green with scum and slime where a thin coating of water trickled from the base of the cave's wall toward the mouth of the cave.

He walked back into the cave a short distance, taking care that no snakes were nesting on the cool stone. As his eyes adjusted, and his ragged breathing slowed, it became obvious that portions of this limestone tunnel were excavated, but there had evidently been no need of shoring. The roof seemed sound, there were no fissures, nor was there any water dripping from the ceiling.

As he proceeded, the tunnel entered the side of a natural cave that had been created by centuries of running water. The process of natural formation had long since ceased, and the limestone was dry and hard.

There was no sign whatever of the dripping, lime-charged water from which stalactites and stalagmites are formed. Nor was there any dark, damp stone beaded along every crack with tiny drops of the yellowish fluid that would signify a live cave. The chemical processes of nature were no longer at work creating new formations. In fact, a mild, cool draught seemed to be drying the chamber.

Sections of the natural tunnel had been widened and squared off by miners. After he'd passed the fork where the tunnel to the rattlesnake's lair lay off to his right, he contin-ued on a short distance into the mountain where he discov-ered a large, man-made room. The ceiling vaulted at least twenty feet above his head, and those who had excavated it had left huge stone columns to support the roof. The columns were about ten feet thick and stood about twenty feet apart in every direction.

The subterranean room he had entered was not entirely dark. Light came down from above, as from a skylight, probably through a vent that had been cut to promote air circulation, but it was still dark enough to be unsettling. As he moved on, it became obvious that he had discovered a combination of natural and man-made tunnels.

CC began speaking loudly in an attempt to dispel the fear that had begun to gnaw at him. When he found himself whistling, he began laughing at himself. The large room produced incredibly clear acoustical effects. He was struck by the beauty of the ceiling. Swirling striations in the ancient flowstone reflected back the dim light.

The floor was relatively flat, with few protrusions, but wavy, like the surface of the sea, and it seemed to rise as he moved away from the tunnel through which he'd entered. As he paced off the perimeter of the room, CC discovered two additional exits. When he reached the far wall, he found another tunnel that led deeper into the mountain. He wondered at the quality of the air until he realized that the miners had cut a number of ventilation shafts above the tunnels. One of these was easily fifteen feet high and sloped uphill. The marks where tools had cut the stone made it obvious that this also was at least partially a man-made tunnel.

In for a penny, in for a pound, he decided, not for the first time. He followed it steeply uphill and, after he walked about fifty yards, he saw daylight leaking through a tangle of vines.

"Not again!" he exclaimed aloud, for he had no desire to get anywhere near those snakes. But he forced himself to continue on, and soon realized that this couldn't be the cave entrance near where the snakes lived because he'd been climbing steadily uphill since entering the caverns.

He started to push his way through the thick tangle of vines when he found himself stepping off into space. If he hadn't grabbed a heavy vine, he'd have gone tumbling to the base of the cliff. In spite of the pain in his chest, he was not about to let go of the vine. He bent his knees until he felt the floor of the tunnel beneath his toes, then pulled himself up until he was able to swing himself back onto the edge of the portal.

After he got his breathing under control, he leaned over the edge enough to estimate the distance to the ground below. He was standing above the mouth of the cave he'd entered the day before, and it was probably a thirty-foot fall to the rocks below.

Stepping gingerly back from the edge, he peered out between the vines that masked the opening. He was looking over the tops of trees that were rooted in the steep slope that ran from the meadow to the stream in the middle of the valley. These trees, along with the vines that masked the caves, would make it nearly impossible for anyone to see this opening, but would at the same time afford him a magnificent view across this end of the valley. He made a mental note to consider taking occasional observations from this point.

Out of the Frying Pan

The Caverns
May 12th, 9:48 a.m.

Wandering back to the main room, he then made his way around its perimeter to the second tunnel. This one appeared to lead back into the mountain.

Following it, he discovered another large chamber, but it didn't approach the size of the one he'd recently explored. At the far side of this chamber, he found a narrow tunnel with sufficient height for him to walk upright. This proved to be a long, winding, natural tunnel. A steady draught of air indicated that sooner or later it must open to the outside.

He wandered on. More chambers and connecting tunnels made him realize that this was an extensive subterranean network, and he had to be careful to turn and look back at every turn to memorize anything distinctive that would help him find his the way back.

Now he understood something of the layout of the caverns that he'd so far explored. He had discovered two entrances beneath the cliffs. If he were able to look down upon them from above, and of course he couldn't, the entrances to the caverns would represent the tops of a huge "Y" laid flat.

He had entered the vine-covered portal to the east, closer to the rattlesnakes, and slightly downhill toward the valley's entrance. The portal through which he'd exited was about fifty yards further west. The two entry tunnels connected, the way the two arms of a "Y" join together at its base, about a hundred paces inside the mountain, and became a single tunnel.

Following that tunnel another hundred paces, he had entered the large underground room. Leaving that room to follow the branch tunnels, he found himself climbing to another portal that opened high above the valley, or entering a confusing labyrinth of tunnels and natural caves that would take him some time to unravel.

He was turning another corner when he slipped on the wet floor. While struggling to maintain his footing, he dropped his flashlight, and was swept with apprehension as he found himself in total darkness.

Perhaps it was a matter of fatigue and his persistent chest pain, but an unreasoning fear quickly filled his consciousness. He'd begun feeling that the mass of the mountain was pressing in on him, suffocating him. Now he found himself squeezing his eyes closed, fighting temporal darkness with physical denial. The plinking of water as it struck the floor, as well as every wayward draft, seemed to signal another danger.

The cavern was no longer a place of refuge for him, but was rapidly becoming a horror hole, and he had to fight to put his fear under. He found himself kneeling in prayer, and his breathing calmed as the specter of evil passed from him. He reached in his pocket for a match, and struck it. Then he

concentrated on what little he could actually see, remembering that believers are to think on those things which are good,
and honest and true, and are not to take counsel of their
fears.

He saw a glint where the match light reflected off the
flashlight laying on the floor of the cave. He retrieved it before the match burned down, but when he pressed the button,
it didn't light. He ran his fingers over the cylinder, and realized that the cap that held the batteries in place was gone.
Lighting another match, he found the cap and two batteries
laying on the ground. He dropped them into his jacket
pocket, then found a piece of paper in another pocket,
twisted it into a spill, and lit it. Holding the burning paper between his fingers, he was able to slip the batteries into the
flashlight and snap the cap back in place. This time, when he
pressed the button, the LED lit.

Although he was still dazzled from staring at the flame,
he got the feeling that this tunnel ran for some distance into
the mountain. As he moved on, galleries opened out on either
side. Some distance ahead, he could see a ray of light, and he
wondered whether this was another vent hole. He shined the
light toward the ceiling. At this point, the tunnel was over
twice his height and had widened to about ten feet. It ran
straight back until lost to sight in the gloom.

He continued on, encouraged by the additional light
from the vent hole, noting that the floor continued to slope
upward as he moved further back into the mountain. From
time to time he passed another gallery on one side or the
other. The place was a labyrinth.

He followed the sound of running water that he heard
coming from the mouth of one of the tunnels. As he worked
his way cautiously along the passageway, the sound grew in
volume until the rock about him seemed to vibrate.

His flashlight batteries were nearly dead, the minimal
light it produced almost useless. He was guiding himself by
running his right hand along the tunnel wall. Something

shifted as his foot struck it, and he bent to discover a rotting piece of wood. A chill passed through him, and he paused to strike one of his few remaining matches.

As he crept forward, the dismal light that it cast seemed to be swallowed by the dark walls, while the glare of the flame effectively blinded him. He tipped the partially consumed match down so that the flames would climb up the yet un-burned wood, then held it down near the floor so that he wasn't completely blinded by the glare. He shuffled on, an in-explicable fear slowing him.

He was so wrapped up in his thoughts that he didn't no-tice the flame reach his fingertips, and he reacted to the pain by dropping the match. His eyes involuntarily traced the path of the dying ember as it dropped toward his feet, but when the glowing match struck the cave floor, it bounced forward, flared to new life, then dropped into a dark crevasse that opened inches in front of his toes.

One glimpse of the abyss he'd been about to step into had been sufficient to paralyze him, and CC found himself swaying forward and back, disoriented by the darkness that seemed even more intense after the flame was extinguished.

Vertigo, born of terror and a lack of visceral orientation, gripped him. Staggering with the dizziness, he sat down abruptly, and kicked one foot out in front of him to push him-self away from the hole. His foot flailed in open space, and he let himself go limp, falling onto his back. Using his elbows to raise his shoulders, he frantically pushed himself away from the hole, crawling crab-like backward, a half dozen feet in the direction from which he had come.

He stopped abruptly. *Suppose I've turned myself around while crawling in the dark? I could be about to push myself over the edge!*

It was only a quarter hour earlier that he'd almost stepped out of the cave entrance into empty space. Now he'd almost stepped off into a hole of undetermined depth. He lay still for a moment, waiting for his breathing to calm, wondering at the providence that had kept him from stepping out over that abyss.

As his eyes grew accustomed to the darkness, he noticed that the tunnel beyond the crevasse was dimly lit from above, a glow so faint that he at first thought it was his imagination. Striking another match, he could see that the chasm before him did not cut off the entire width of the tunnel, but just the right side where he'd been walking. Dropping the match, and lighting another, he moved carefully around the perimeter of the hole, then moved up the left side of the cavern.

When time permits, and especially if anyone ever joins me here, I'll need to build a safety railing around that hole.

The light grew stronger as he found himself moving steeply downhill, and in a few minutes he entered a large room. It only took a moment before he realized he'd come full circle, and was again near the portal by which he'd entered.

He was certain of one thing. He'd had enough of this cavern for the time being. When and if he returned, he would carry more than one flashlight, as well as a can of fluorescent spray paint to label the various tunnel intersections and rooms. As he shuffled along, he found himself intoning over and over again in a hoarse whisper, "Thank you, Lord."

A Subterranean Warehouse

The Lower Limestone Cave
May 12th, 1:10 p.m.

After exiting the cave, he sat down on a boulder to try to relieve the pain he was experiencing from moving about with injured ribs.

After a few minutes of staring dumbly at the ground, he glanced around the meadow. His eyes widened when he no-ticed what looked like a concrete platform adjacent to the cave's portal. A moss-covered ramp led along the face of the

cliff from the mouth of the cave up to the top of the platform.

He rose to his feet and walked over to take a closer look.
Standing beside it, he pressed his finger to his side to mark its
height, then walked back through the woods to the tractor-
trailer where he checked his crude measurement against the
height of its tailgate. The platform and the deck of the truck
were almost exactly the same height.

Excited now, he opened one of the trailer's doors and
managed to lift down a step ladder he'd left at the back of the
trailer. Leaning the ladder against the deck of the truck, he
climbed up into the trailer, located a rake and a shovel among
the garden tools at the rear of the rig, and tossed them to the
ground. Then he gingerly climbed back down to the ground,
carried the tools back to the platform, and began slowly
scraping the mulch away.

He experienced severe pain when he tried to move too
rapidly, or when he tried to stretch too far, but the leafy compost proved easy enough to scrape off the flaking concrete
surface of the ramp.

Returning to the trailer, he opened both rear doors, fastened them back to the outside of the trailer, then made his
way to the cab.

Thank God that this thing has power steering! he thought. He
slowly turned the rig around, taking special care not to drop a
wheel into one of those trenches that crisscrossed much of the
meadow.

Backing the trailer toward the platform, he wondered
how long it had been since the limestone operation had closed
down. It was obvious that the trees beneath the cliff had
grown a good deal during the years since. *These workings must
be nearly a hundred years old,* he thought. "And that's how old I
feel right now," he added aloud with asperity.

It took him several tries before he backed squarely to the
platform, backing into it twice before finally lining the trailer
up. When he walked to the back of the trailer he discovered

that its floor was about four inches above the level of the platform.

He marked where the wheels of the trailer were setting,
pulled it ahead a couple of yards, and dug shallow holes for
the wheels. When he backed up again, the wheels dropped
into the holes, but the trailer bed was still about two inches
above the level of the platform. He pulled the truck ahead
again, and dug down a little deeper. It was painful work because many small tree roots ran through the soil. Finally, his
breath coming in gasps, he backed the truck up again and felt
it settle squarely against the old loading dock.

I'm done for the day, he thought. *Time to celebrate.* He opened
a can of stew, ate it cold, swallowed a pain pill with some water, wrapped himself in a blanket, and simply collapsed across
the truck seat.

When the sunlight awakened him he felt little better, but
knew he had to finish this task. He ate some canned fruit,
then walked slowly out to the edge of the trees to make certain no one was nearby. After scanning the area and listening
for any tell-tale sounds, he returned to the trailer.

He walked slowly up the ancient concrete ramp, crossed
the platform, entered the back of the trailer and climbed onto
the forklift machine. It started immediately, its propane fueled
engine operating smoothly. It had been parked with the forks
beneath a pallet of boxes. He raised it a few inches, put it in
reverse, and slowly backed off onto the platform.

A little frightened of working on an inclined surface, he
backed slowly down the long ramp, turned into the cave, and
drove about a hundred feet to the main chamber. He set the
pallet down a few feet from the right-hand wall, then drove
back to the trailer and shut down the forklift.

It won't do, he thought, *to have that yellow gum ball light flash-
ing continually, much less having it producing those loud warning chirps.*

Locating a screwdriver and pliers in the cab of the truck,
he tracked the wires that powered the safety devices and cut
them.

I'm the only one here, he thought, *and I don't plan to drive the forklift over myself.*

After all the painful experiences he'd had, he enjoyed operating the fork lift. In spite of the distance up and down the tunnel, he still had the entire trailer unloaded in less than two hours. Leaving the forklift in the main cave, he went back out to the truck.

Leaning back, he pressed his hands in the small of his back, and groaned. Everything seemed to hurt. He noticed that the sky had turned a threatening gray, and decided he'd better get the truck out of sight before the ground was turned to mud. Without hesitation, and for what he now knew was truly the last time, he turned the key in the ignition of the huge truck. He drove slowly because, even with the benefit of power steering, his ribs hurt when he raised his arms or tried to turn the wheel. He pulled forward between the trees, did a broken U-turn, and pulled the truck around so that the cab pointed at the mouth of the cave.

Approaching the cliff, he lined it up with the mouth of the tunnel. Then he turned on the headlights and pulled into the dark opening. About thirty yards up the tunnel, he turned the wheel to pass around a supporting column, got too near one wall of the tunnel, and felt his chest slam against the truck's steering wheel as the rig came to a screeching halt. He shook his head in self-reproach, and wryly observed to himself that he hadn't double-checked the roof height.

Morphed photos, ©2014, Frank Becker

Climbing down and moving around the front bumper, he saw in the reflection from the headlights that the upper right corner of the trailer had been crushed where he'd rammed it into a protruding shelf of rock. Walking back to the driver's side, he commented sourly, "Well, I've got plenty of room on this side." Looking toward the tunnel portal, he realized that he'd already pulled far enough around the curve that the trailer was out of sight of anyone who might be standing outside. If, however, they were to walk very far into the cave, they'd undoubtedly spot it.

"Almost done," he thought, as he walked slowly back down the tunnel. When he reached the woods, he started to kick pine needles into the tire ruts, but wound up holding his side because of the pain. So he took out his pocketknife, whittled off a pine branch, and used it as a broom to smooth needles over the holes he'd dug for the wheels. He had just turned back toward the tunnel when there was an explosion of thunder, and a torrent of rain struck him. He made his way back to the tunnel as quickly as he could move.

In his wet clothes, the ice-box effect of the cavern chilled him, and he realized that he would have to be careful to avoid pneumonia and other respiratory ailments while living in that dank atmosphere. Perhaps he'd later mull over the wonder of parking the tractor-trailer completely underground, but it didn't seem very pleasant here, particularly in contrast to the beautiful early May weather he'd been experiencing.

Having returned to his cache, CC began reading carton labels until he located a box of clothing. Donning a sweater and knit cap, he made his way back to the cab, assembled his portable cook stove, heated a can of baked beans, and cut up a can of Boston brown bread. He'd wolfed down several bites before some impulse made him set down his spoon. He then bowed his head to confess his ingratitude to God for his incredible provision.

He knew that the discovery of the caverns should have produced a sense of relief and inner peace, but in the ensuing hours, he'd found himself fighting the same fear of discovery and enslavement that he'd been living with for the past month. It was as if he were in a prison from which he could not motivate himself to move, even though the cell door was wide open.

He reasoned that it would take some time before he would feel free of anxiety. He would probably never rid himself of a certain amount of concern, but that concern would serve to make him more careful, and might help to keep him alive.

"On the other hand," he laughed, "I don't want to die young from worry-induced ulcers."

He was like Peter in prison. *Would an angel have to smite me to get me to shift my thinking?* he wondered.

The pain in his ribs, when he laughed or took a deep breath, made him even more aware of his tenuous situation. He remembered God's word. "Be anxious for nothing, but in everything by prayer and supplication with thanksgiving let your requests be made known to God." And his mind went off in another direction. *Why am I able to quote that passage?*

He burned the paper plate from which he'd eaten, laughing ironically at his use of this 21st Century throw-away. It was an irreplaceable luxury from another age, an age that had ended just a month before. Since, however, he'd packed thousands of them, it seemed wise to use them until he was equipped to properly wash dishes.

A Temporary Camp

The Lower Limestone Cave
May 12th, 11:30 a.m.

CC didn't want to sleep in the caverns, at least not yet. While he was unloading the trailer, he'd used the forklift to spread the stacks of cartons and equipment out over a large area, stacking them in low piles on wooden pallets, so that he wouldn't have to move a lot of cartons to locate something he might need. Now he walked among the stacks to make his selections and began carrying those items to the portal.

Just outside the cave's entrance he set up a large camouflaged dome tent, furnishing it with a cot, sleeping bag, and other necessary gear. Then he cleared a space for his fire pit just inside the entrance, making certain any flames would be well shielded from prying eyes. He wanted the pleasure of camping while preparing a more permanent and healthy home within the cave. He'd keep an eye on the radiation meter, but he was convinced that the heavier particles had dropped from the clouds, and he was in a relatively low risk area.

Several pain-filled trips to his stock pile provided him with a variety of food, clothing, cleaning supplies, and a shot gun. He took a pain reliever, and though it was only mid-afternoon, he lay down on his cot fully clothed and tried to get some sleep. His chest hurt whenever he moved, and carrying the gear out of the cave had not helped. The pain from his cracked rib seemed to be causing muscle spasms throughout his upper body.

He tossed and turned for a half hour, and found it impossible to sleep. His head buzzed with pain, but also with ideas. After a while he drifted into a troubled sleep, but awoke again in late afternoon, weak and sick, and just able to open one of his bottles of water. He had been alternately soaked with sweat, then shaken with chills, and he lay on the cot, listless and a bit frightened. Finally dropping off into an exhausted sleep, he didn't wake until the following morning.

Ruminations

The Lower Limestone Cave
May 12th, 8 p.m.

The helplessness he felt as a result of his fall from the tree, coupled with his generally rundown condition, served to underline how vulnerable he was to any exigencies. Although he felt somewhat stronger, when the sky again threatened rain he moved his gear back inside the portal, leaving the tent where it was until he had strength to deal with it.

That evening he sat on a folding chair just inside the mouth of the cavern, enjoying the sound of the heavy rainfall. Warmly dressed, and with a small fire burning cheerfully at his feet, he peered out into darkness. The ordinary night sounds of loon and owl, bullfrog and fox, were stilled by the rain, for each had sought his own shelter.

CC found the steady downpour restful, aware that few creatures, including man, were apt to be out roaming about, and he was relatively secure in his rock shelter. His only concern was whether the rattlesnakes had taken refuge on higher ground because of flooding in their holes, and he occasionally cast his eyes about, looking for signs that they might be drawn to his fire.

The smoldering embers in his makeshift fireplace cast weird shadows over the cave walls, and the sharp odors of damp pine and woodland humus mingled with the rich scents of burning wood and percolating coffee. He was warm, dry and comfortable.

Contrasting his own circumstance with those he imagined most survivors were experiencing, he went from a feeling of smug satisfaction to one of near guilt because of what he considered his misplaced pride and casual indifference to their sufferings. The things that had happened to him could not be explained by luck, ability, or good looks. *Especially not by good looks,* he thought wryly.

He'd set a radiation detector just inside the cave's portal so that it was out of the rain, and was pleased to see that it indicated no significant radiation. This was not nuclear rain — a phrase he'd coined to describe the precipitation whose raindrops formed around particles of radioactive dust, bringing to earth a combination of life-giving moisture and death-dealing radiation.

In his loneliness, and his inability to share ideas and concerns with another human being, he was given increasingly to a black, cynical humor. Still, when and if these rains finally cleared the skies, then perhaps the sun would shine clearly again. The downside was that when the stratosphere finally purged itself of the dust, the radioactive material would have washed into earthen hollows and the beds of streams, forming pockets of radiation.

These toxins would enter the food chain, first absorbed by the grasses, then eaten by birds and animals, and finally entering humans through the milk and meat those animals produced. With careful husbandry, however, crops might once again grow in nonpoisonous soil, farm animals might flourish, and people might move safely within carefully delineated areas. Until then, he would continue to watch his radiation meters and try to stay alive.

He thought of the rains. During the first few days following the war, incredible meteorological spectacles had torn the earth. Rains, snows, and fierce winds — hot and cold — had ripped the planet, shattering the earth's atmosphere and confounding communications. Erratic radio reports indicated that large areas of the world had been devastated by hurricanes, tornadoes, and tsunamis.

There appeared to be two reasons why the damage from nuclear weapons wasn't more extensive, and why "nature" responded so violently to help clean up the mess. First, strange electronic phenomenon in the atmosphere foiled the plans of the war-makers, causing some missiles to abort and their warheads not to detonate.

Second, radical weather conditions reduced the damage by washing the radioactive fallout from the earth and skies.

Third, at great personal risk, some military leaders among the various aggressors simply refused to fire the weapons for which they were responsible. Many were labeled traitors, and later probably stood before firing squads for their noble actions.

The initial explosions produced microwaves that damaged the weapons systems of nearby planes and missiles by erasing their computers' memories. As a result, countless weapons had malfunctioned.

It might have been different if only one enemy had fired missiles, for they could have carefully timed their targeting so that they didn't interfere with one another. With multiple attacks from various antagonists occurring unexpectedly, that was not possible.

Those same microwave explosions also destroyed the scores of computers built into the hundreds of millions of automobiles and trucks that had been built since the 1970s, rendering them inoperable, and leaving their owners on foot.

That explained the untold number of cars that were abandoned wherever they suddenly stalled.

Immediately following the initial nuclear attacks, there was a tremendous natural upheaval in the stratosphere that caused a huge cold air mass to move down from the Arctic, sweeping the nuclear fallout east across the southern United States, Western Europe, and Asia.

The reason for the irregular fallout pattern was easy to explain but impossible to forecast. The bombs that exploded at the earth's surface, "dirty bombs," scooped up huge quantities of earth, irradiated it, and created incalculable amounts of fallout that endangered every living thing for thousands of miles downwind. The explosive force of a five-megaton warhead — equivalent to five-million tons of dynamite — swept the dirt up to as high as twenty miles above the earth. Stratospheric winds carried this fallout in a west to east direction, blowing it in unpredictable patterns over the surface of the earth.

Rogue nations, intent on maliciously destroying America, used dirty bombs, detonating them near the earth's surface, and scooping up millions of tons of earth that ultimately became the fallout which endangered the population downwind.

Major powers intent on world domination, however, used "clean bombs." Their warheads were cleaner in the sense that the radioactive cores they employed had shorter half-lives, and they detonated them high above the earth's surface, thus killing multitudes, while producing less fallout.

One broadcast stated that Russia had dropped Neutron Bombs on Washington DC, New York, Houston, Chicago, and L.A., with the intent that the radiation would wipe out the populace while leaving the structures of America's largest cities relatively undamaged. These buildings, after a relatively short time, would be safe for occupation by whichever invaders were able to get there first.

As early as the Cuban missile crisis of the 1960's, U.S. civil defense authorities had been producing maps indicating the geographic areas most likely to be heavily blanketed by fallout.

Following the initial hostilities, word had gone out by ham radio operators that the northern Great Plains, northern New England, and eastern Canada and its Maritime Provinces were the cleanest areas in North America. In consequence, many of the survivors in the crowded northeast corridor had begun a trek toward New England, the majority dying en route.

CC was bemused that people were moving to northern New England because — after a major volcanic eruption in Indonesia in 1816 and the subsequent worldwide drop in temperatures and resultant massive crop failures — people had left the northeast en masse.

Now, however, the weather had become completely unpredictable. It was as though God was pouring out His judgment, and the heavens were weeping for those who had the temerity to pervert his gifts.

Freak storms heaped deep spring snow over the Rockies and as far south as Texas, killing countless numbers of the original survivors and much of the remaining livestock. Spectacular thunderstorms poured several feet of rain over most of the North American continent, unexpectedly cleansing the skies of much of the heavier and more dangerous fallout, and concentrating it in the depths of certain river systems. Wherever the fallout was washed into deep water, its radiation was effectively shielded by the mass of the water above it. The fish that lived off any plants and animals growing there, however, would be deadly fare.

While nuclear war had long posed an enormous threat to all, the long-term damage of a single detonation had been oversold by the anti-war element, and had terrorized most Americans. He remembered reading that the radiation from the nuclear tests made on the Eniwetok Atoll in the Pacific during the 1950s had proven damaging to those who were exposed. Thyroid tumors began appearing among the native people who had been exposed to the 1954 tests. Among the young, there was also a higher than normal incidence of growth retardation.

Yet scientists were later amazed at how quickly nature recovered. It was assumed that the radiation would prove so potent that no life — plant, animal, or fish — would be able to exist there for thousands of years. It was assumed that whatever life might survive would likely be misshapen and grotesque, because their cells would be damaged by the radiation.

In fact, within just a generation the undersea life — plant and animal — had resumed its normal course, and there appeared to be no significant long-term damage. CC had examined the photographs of the Eniwetok Atoll, showing a myriad of healthy sea life, and was encouraged that all might not be lost.

He had read on, and learned that further scientific testing had shown that, throughout history, the race has been continually bombarded by radiation from the earth and the sky.

He was intrigued to learn that passengers on jet airliners flying in the thin atmosphere at 30,000 feet absorbed significant dangerous radiation through their aluminum hulls during daylight hours. That's why many trans flights are made during the hours of darkness.

What's more, millions drinking "pure" water from deep wells often received more radiation from that water than was received by those living next to nuclear power plants. Scientists also discovered that radioactive radon gas, seeping through basement and cellar floors, had resulted in countless deaths from cancer.

CC's studies led him to realize that radiation has been with us since the beginning of time. In light of the radical increase in radiation over the short term, his task was to limit his exposure and hope for the best. He knew that some of the phenomenal events occurring around the world might have both a positive and negative impact.

Unexplained earthquakes fractured the southwestern and northeastern United States, leveling cities and even rerouting rivers. And Yellowstone National Park suffered a volcanic eruption that almost overnight created a mountain a mile high over what had been the caldera of an enormous volcano, and multiplying the pollutants in the atmosphere. It seemed reasonable to conclude that the shocks from the atomic bombs precipitated quakes in already unstable faults in the earth's crust.

The storms killed multitudes of already weakened survivors who were unable to find shelter. Some of those sheltering underground were drowned, but those who survived came out under cleaner and safer skies than they might otherwise have anticipated.

Disease and bacteria wreaked havoc where the dead lay legion, for most people were unprepared for any sort of disaster and had simply gone home and perished within the confines of their own walls. Millions succumbed out of ignorance and because of their failure to prepare for emergencies.

The rains that had followed the war were frequent, frightening and torrential. The ground was sodden. Even in the east, flash flooding became a constant danger to the unwary traveler. It was as though God was determined to purge the world of the evidence of man's stupidity, and many Christians wondered whether this presaged the return of the Lord.

Thus the rainy weather outside his cave made CC's humble home seem relatively secure and luxurious. The water that dripped down from the cliff above the portal made a snapping bubbling sound as it fell to the sloping stone floor at the entrance, working a syncopated rhythm with the steady drumming of the rain on the leaves of the forest. The stream in which he'd swum when he first entered the valley had become a raging torrent.

In the past, camping would have been a wonderful vacation experience, but it was no longer so for CC. This was not recreation. He was subject to the dangers of exposure to the elements as well as from other human beings. He had come to fear the very society he craved and needed. His physical condition, particularly his cracked ribs, kept him from undertaking any meaningful work. He had planned to construct his little cottage within the large, relatively dry chamber in the cavern, but though he had been able to unload the tractor-trailer using the forklift, he was in no condition to open the packages of lumber that made up the garage, or begin to build any kind of a permanent home.

Yet he had to get under cover — and into a warm, dry shelter — for he was exposing himself to respiratory infections. Since he did not yet have the strength to build his home, he'd moved into the sleeper cab of the truck, but both the truck and the cave were damp, cold, and depressing.

He was resting in the truck's cab one evening about four days after his fall, when an idea came to him. A tourist map he'd found in a rack at the book store in Deep River Junction had indicated that there was both a farmer's co-op and a tavern on the isolated stretch of highway somewhere north of this valley. The ad for the co-op advertised everything from farm supplies to recreation vehicles. It seemed to him that if he could get an RV up here and into the cave, he'd be a lot more comfortable.

Reconnaissance

The Lower Limestone Cave
May 16th, 8:40 a.m.

CC's chest still occasionally pained him, but he thought it was time to reconnoiter outside his little valley. He'd searched through the pallets of supplies and equipment he'd brought in on the truck, and it didn't take him long to find what he was looking for. On the edge of one pallet, he'd tied a fully assembled electric bicycle that he'd found at the sporting goods store.

The bike didn't look a lot different from the fat-tired bikes of the 1940's, but there were significant differences. This bike could be pedaled, but it also had a battery and an electric motor that would enable him to ride up to a distance of thirty miles at twenty miles per hour. And whenever he did pedal, he would be recharging the battery. It appeared to be great transportation for someone who hadn't fully recovered his strength.

He set the assembled bike on the cave floor. Rummaging through a carton, he found several cans of spray paint which were left over from camouflaging the tractor-trailer. He hated to spoil this beautiful new bicycle, but he needed to lower its visibility so he rolled it outside the tunnel and sprayed over the entire bike, covering its bright yellow paint job with an ir-regular pattern of tan, green, and gray. He even sprayed the chrome and tires, hoping to reduce all reflection and break up any geometric lines. While the paint was drying, he ate supper and packed a few things. There was no telling how long he might be gone, so he decided to carry enough food for two days.

He filled the saddlebags with his emergency rations, then added a first-aid kit and a couple of water-filled plastic bot-tles. Instead of a sleeping bag, he carried a Mylar space blan-ket in which he could wrap himself to keep warm. He had been carrying a small emergency kit on his belt. It contained a surgical face mask, swimming goggles, disposable gloves, waterproofed matches, a space blanket, a compass, a package of pain relievers, and a jackknife. He never went anywhere without it. And, of course, he wore a radiation detection badge on his jacket.

He left the cave and was well down the old log road be-fore dusk. As he reached the middle of his valley, the sun was so low in the west that the upper end of the valley where he now lived was already in deep shadows, while the woods at the mouth of the valley were bathed in a golden light. As he reached the trees within the bottleneck, it seemed particularly dark, so he walked the bike.

Just before he reached the highway, he stopped beneath the cover of the evergreens. Since the state road was to the east of the tall cliffs, it was already in deep shadow, but the sun still cast its light across the top of the cliffs, lighting the far side of the valley below him. He stood under cover and waited for the sun to sink. The massive shadow seemed to slide toward him as it eclipsed the valley below, seeming to consume it.

In the growing darkness, he could see a farmhouse on the far side of the valley, lights twinkling in the windows, and he wondered whether it might be an outpost for an unknown enemy. In spite of his fear, nostalgia nearly overwhelmed him as he gazed at the peaceful setting.

Now that he was on the road, he was apprehensive that a vehicle might appear from either direction. He looked south, back up the hill toward Deep River Junction. The highway was dark and silent. Then he turned his eyes toward the north. Although the sun was down, there was still enough afterglow to see far down the hill where the highway disappeared in a wide curve to the left.

Mounting the bike, he coasted slowly downhill, keeping his speed in check by riding the brakes. He estimated that he'd coasted about a mile before he neared the bottom of the long hill. The sense of freedom he was experiencing reminded him of the first time he'd ever ridden a bicycle, but when he tried to picture the actual occasion, it eluded him.

Can't think about that now. Got to concentrate on the task at hand. Memories will return to me in time. They've got to!

Coasting down that long hill was easy enough, but when he reached level ground and started to pedal the bike, his side began to hurt. He rotated the right hand grip to send power to the rear wheel, the bike accelerated quickly, and he enjoyed an amazing sense of freedom.

He had been thinking that it would be fun to try the bike in the ditch alongside the road, but visibility was poor, and he dared not risk an accident. Then discretion gave way to necessity because a vehicle was racing down the mountain behind him, its headlights sweeping the highway as it approached. Braking as hard as he dared, he steered the bike over the shoulder and down into the ditch beside the road.

He was astonished at the way the bike ran down the side of the swale and tracked through the mud and shallow water. In the gloom, he spotted a small culvert pipe that drained the ditch. He slid up alongside it, dropped the bike on its side, and threw himself down below the wall just before the car shot by.

After it passed, he looked up to see whether the driver slowed, but the tail lights didn't brighten. He quickly rolled the bike out of the ditch, and was annoyed to find that the seat was slick with mud and water. Then he realized that it didn't matter. He had obviously sat in the puddle himself. He mounted the bike and pedaled slowly forward. The question was, would the battery and motor be shorted out?

The answer came quickly enough. When he twisted the hand grip, the bike accelerated up the hill, evidently none the worse for its brief partial immersion. He was grateful for the self-powered bike, for he was more exhausted than he'd realized. The evening breeze was mild for May in central Vermont, and being wet and muddy, he was enjoying himself immensely. The stars had come out, and though the moon had not yet risen, he was able to see enough to stay in the roadway.

It was his first trip out of the valley, and he did not realize how much he'd missed his mobility. He was lost in thought when he noticed that there was a break in the shadows and the trees on his right began to thin.

Green Mountain Feed & Grain Store

Central Vermont

May 16th, about 8 p.m.

He was several miles north of Hidden Valley when he finally found the place. Even by starlight it was obviously a very old, ill-kept building, its gutters dragging and shutters askew. Joined to the store on its right was a brick warehouse with large, old-fashioned swinging doors.

There were no night lights burning, and CC concluded that the entire eastern U.S. electrical grid was down and would probably remain out of operation for months, perhaps forever. He had an LED lamp strapped to his forehead, and he selected the red light option. It wouldn't be visible at any distance, but would provide sufficient illumination to help him find his way around.

He moved toward the right corner of the building where someone had tacked a large hand-made poster to a sign post. Using a black felt marker, they had drawn a skull and cross-bones, and below it printed a warning. "This facility is under the protection of the Home Guard. Trespassers will be shot on sight."

CC stifled a laugh. *It's appropriate that the so-called "Home Guard" would use a skull and crossbones to symbolize their piratical claim. Kind of dumb,* he thought. *This place is so run down that if they hadn't brought attention to it by posting this warning, most people would pass by without a second glance.*

Flicking off the headlamp, he examined the front of the building by moonlight. The store itself had a gabled roof. The paint on it's trim was peeling, and a gutter was hanging from the fascia, but the building had a substantial stone foundation and the slate roof looked in good repair. The warehouse had a sign above the door advertising seed and grain. On the gravel drive were two pumps, one for regular gasoline and the other for diesel. It was obvious that the business had been barely able to survive under the socialistic burdens placed upon it by Washington.

In order to ride his bike around the left side of the store, he had to pass a small copse of trees and brush. Rounding the corner to the far side, he discovered a propane gas filling station and a large parking lot overgrown with weeds. He pushed his bike to the back of the store, and laid it against the side of a sloped door that accessed the cellar.

Straightening up, he looked out across the parking area. He smiled. A used motor home was parked in a patch of weeds with a "For Sale" sign taped over the windshield. He walked over and tried the doors, but found both locked. One of the door handles showed evidence of tampering where someone had left scratch marks, presumably trying to force the lock.

CC ran to the rear of the store and tried the door marked "Deliveries Only." It too was locked. It was constructed of heavy planks, strapped with steel bands. The windows weren't boarded over, but even stretching to his full height, he could barely reach their bottom sills. And if he could have reached them, he didn't want to break in because he wanted to leave as little evidence of his visit as possible. He returned to the outside ramped cellar door, and discovered that the hasp had not been secured with a padlock. He was about to lift the doors when he thought he heard the sound of a shoe scraping on the ground nearby.

Fear seized him as he realized that he might be captured and shot for looting. Forcing himself to remain calm, he dropped to his knees next to the sloped basement door to lessen his silhouette. He waited quietly for several minutes before deciding that what he'd heard must have been a branch brushing against something.

He stood, flipped the hasp, lifted the doors, and stepped onto the concrete stairway that led down to the cellar. When he reached the bottom of the stairs, he found another unlocked door. Pushing it open, he stepped quickly into the cellar, pushed the door closed behind him, then turned on his headlamp to examine the room.

There was an oil burner and a 275-gallon oil tank in the corner to his left, and a sump hole to his right. He couldn't see across the cellar because, except for the staircase to the main floor, the remainder of the basement was crowded with cartons stacked from floor to ceiling on wooden palettes.

He began reading the labels, then opened a couple to examine their contents. He found gourmet foods, upscale clothing, medical supplies and drugs, as well as cases of guns and ammunition. He was stunned by the magnitude of the cache, and realized that this was a treasure trove of items that had been systematically stolen and stockpiled by a well-organized group. That meant that his being there was far more dangerous than he'd imagined.

Well, I'm here now, he thought, *so, once again, "In for a penny, in for a pound. Or, for those who are not English,* he smiled, *"In for a penny, in for a dollar."*

He climbed the inside cellar stairs to the ground floor, and found that the door at the top was also unlocked. *Is it that they are so trusting,* he wondered, *or that most survivors are now under their control?*

Working his way to the front of the store, he looked for anything of value. He checked the open cash register, and checked under the counter, but found little of interest. Then he noticed a keyboard on the wall behind the counter. The black print on the labels didn't show up in the red light, so he flicked on the clear white lights. He examined the labels, one at a time, until he found a set of keys marked "motor home," and slipped them into his pocket.

He wandered around the store and began selecting items that he stacked near the front door. Back in the hardware section, he picked up a roll of hardware cloth and another of window screen. In the automobile aisle, he found a large roll of fiberglass cloth, and a stack of gallon cans of automotive body putty. In the paint section, he picked up two gallons of flat paint, one gray and one tan. Then he unlocked the front door from the inside and began carrying the items out to the motor home, piling them on the ground by the door.

The motor home key was stiff in the lock, but after he worked it gently back and forth, the bolt slipped back. He began stacking everything on the floor, starting at the back of the motor home. Then he went back to the cache in the cellar, gathered two semi-automatic rifles, a thousand rounds of ammunition, assorted camouflage suits, a variety of medical supplies, and a quantity of drugs, including antibiotics and pain-killers. Cartons containing a variety of medical instruments caught his attention, and were added to the growing stack.

He was growing weary from the trips up and down the cellar stairs, but was willing to make the effort because he didn't want to miss the opportunity to pick up cases of molasses, maple syrup, and honey, along with assorted jams, juices, and fruits. He also took a case of canned hams. He had decided to carry these heavy articles up the outside cellar stairs to save steps, but after a dozen trips, he was exhausted, and his chest was aching again. When he finally moved them to the motor home, the cartons filled the hallway and kitchen floor area.

Locking the front door of the store from the inside, CC went back down through the cellar, exiting the way he'd entered. Pulling the door closed behind him, and inserting a peg in the hasp, he climbed the stairs and closed the sloping doors at the top. It was a relief to be finished inside the building.

He returned to the motor home and slid behind the wheel. When he turned the key in the ignition, he heard a few clicks from the starter solenoid, then there was silence. The battery was dead.

Since there was no electricity at the store, there could be no way to recharge the battery. He was stuck, and he had to get back to the valley before dawn. He still had his electric bike, of course, but he'd have to leave everything else behind.

Not only would he have failed in his purpose, but he'd have made it obvious that someone had attempted to rob the store.

Dejected, he was pushing his bike away from the building when the crescent moon broke through the clouds, casting its light across a sign hanging on the left side of the building. "Gasoline."

Of course, it's a gas station! And where there is gasoline, there are often other automotive products. Like oil. And antifreeze. And batteries!

He rode the bike back to the motor home, then walked back toward the cellar doors. Half way there, he snapped his fingers, then turned and jogged back to the motor home. *Where on earth do they put a battery in a motor home,* he wondered. He had to risk the flashlight. It was a scene too familiar to troubled motorists. He found the battery compartment under the hood, next to the engine, and leaned in to check its size.

Returning to the basement door, he again worked his way through the cellar to the first floor. No auto batteries! He saw a sign above a side door that read "Feed and Grain." He made his way through the door into the adjacent warehouse. Large burlap and paper bags were stacked on pallets, with miscellaneous tools and equipment hanging along the side walls. He found what he was looking for in the rear corner, an assortment of batteries. He sorted through a box of tools, grabbed a few wrenches, shoved them into his hip pocket, and carried the heavy battery to the motor home.

It took all his strength to lift the battery up onto the fender, and he felt as though he'd again strained his injured ribs while getting the old battery out and replacing it with the new one. With the cable clamps tightly connected, he slid down to the bumper, secured the hood, then dropped to the ground, gasping from the pain.

Climbing painfully back into the driver's compartment, he prayed that the battery still held a charge. He turned the key. The engine immediately started, then died. "Please, Lord," he muttered. He pumped the gas once, leaned forward and turned the key again, and the engine caught. He sat there for nearly a minute, keeping the engine at a high idle. When he was reasonably confident that it would continue running, he returned to the cellar.

Just as he reached the bottom of the inside stairway, he heard the cellar door slam behind him. Before he could reach it, someone on the outside rammed something into the hasp to secure it. He turned and raced back up the inside stairway to the main floor, only to discover that his antagonist had already managed to get inside the building and lock the door at the top of the stairs as well. CC was trapped.

He heard what sounded like a motorcycle engine start, then the sound of tires spinning as it raced away. It seemed certain that his would-be captor would soon return with reinforcements, but he didn't intend to be there when they arrived. Using his flashlight, he soon discovered a stack of rusting garden tools behind the oil furnace.

Picking up a sledge hammer, he half ran, half staggered to the cellar door. Ignoring the tearing pain in his chest, he swung the heavy hammer at the point where the lock met the jamb. He put all of his pent-up frustration into the blow, and the hammer smashed the door open. Then he was up the outside stairs and walking as rapidly as he could toward the motor home.

When he released his breath, the pain caught at him, and he made a futile effort to breathe shallowly. He whispered a prayer of thanks that his assailant had not thought to shut down the motor home engine, nor remove the keys from the ignition. He somehow got the heavy electric bike up into the motor home, slammed the door, and climbed behind the wheel.

CC had originally planned to tape over each headlamp with duct tape, leaving only a narrow horizontal slit by which to see the road, but there was no time. He turned on the headlights, pulled the lever on the automatic transmission into reverse, backed around the vacant lot onto the highway, then turned up the mountain road.

Surprisingly, the trip back to his valley was uneventful. He entered the bottleneck at a little after three, and after brushing out the signs of his passing he drove directly to the west end of the valley. There he drove the motor home into the cave, pulled it up past the tractor-trailer, and shut it down on the levelest spot he could find.

With the interior lights on, he got a casual look at the RV. Although it was beautiful, he didn't take time to examine it. He didn't even bother with bedding, just turned off the lights, lowered himself onto one of the twin beds in the rear bedroom, and fell asleep.

Camouflaging the Cave

Hidden Valley

May 19th, 8:40 a.m.

CC arose early, excited about the challenge he'd set for himself. After four days of light labor, unpacking and caring for the items that he'd carried back in the motor home, and with his chest pain nearly gone, he wanted to do what he could to secure his hideaway.

After breakfast, he picked up a saw and an ax, and wandered to the far edge of the woods where he spent some time looking down the valley for any sign of life. When he was satisfied that there was no one around, he went back into the heart of the woods and cut down a half-dozen saplings.

Stripping them of their branches, he dragged the refuse into a pile beneath the low-hanging boughs of an evergreen. Then he brushed mud over the newly cut stumps to disguise them, and made several trips to drag the poles back to the cave. Mild pain was warning him to ease up, so he made himself a hot meal and spent the remainder of the day reading.

The next morning he dragged the saplings about thirty feet inside the cave's entrance where, even at midday, the light was poor. He built a sort of fence by crisscrossing the poles from wall to wall and ceiling to floor. He cut them to length and, where possible, he put the ends in niches in the rock, bending them slightly so that the tension tended to keep them in position. Wherever they criss-crossed, he wired them together, creating a grid with the saplings. The result looked like a floor-to-ceiling fence. This took the better part of a day, and effectively closed off the entire cave.

The following morning, he installed a small door and frame, complete with hinges, in the lower left corner of the wall. After lunch he returned to the job, using heavy staples to fasten half-inch hardware cloth over the entire surface. This heavy mesh fencing, often used for cages for small animals, stiffened the wall. Now, even a rabbit couldn't squirm through.

On the third morning, he began wiring window screen atop the entire surface of hardware cloth, carefully shaping it to simulate the striations in the existing tunnel walls. Then he began experimenting with small quantities of the auto body putty he'd found at the co-op, spreading it in a thin layer over the screened surface, molding it to look like the cavern walls, and carefully blending it where it met those walls.

The artificial wall now covered the entire cross-section of the tunnel, with the edges of the doorway irregularly shaped so that it was nearly invisible in the near darkness. He found himself coughing from the chemicals in the air, but persisted as he applied a second coat of epoxy, building up layer on layer.

He dug up a quantity of dry sand from the cave floor, sand that had been eroded over the years. Then he applied a mixture of gray and tan paint to his wall that closely matched the color of the tunnel walls. He then textured his wall by throwing handfuls of the dry sand against the wet paint. When he had finished, he was satisfied that, in the dark tunnel, all but the most careful observer would assume that his artificial wall was actually the back end of a cave.

Explorations

West end of the valley

May 21st, 8:45 a.m.

Breathing the fumes from the fiberglass compound had left CC short of breath — nauseous and lethargic. He puttered about the motor home the next day, heating soup for lunch, and generally resting.

He was frustrated because he'd made long lists of things he wanted to accomplish each day, and he was falling behind. His single accomplishment for the day was limited to running a long wire from the antenna on the motor home's sophisticated radio down the cave to the hardware cloth that closed off the cavern. As it happened, it made a superb antenna.

The following day, in spite of occasional chest pains, he decided to do a little more exploring. He packed a lunch, filled an empty water bottle with spring water that flowed from the cliff near his cave, picked up his rifle, and headed west through the woods.

It was becoming his habit to start early, as people had for centuries, adjusting their living patterns to the rising and setting of the sun because of the need for natural light. Beneath the towering cliffs there was still a chill in the air, but he'd eaten a good breakfast and dressed warmly, so he felt adequately fortified for this morning's adventures.

Breakfast had been special. Using the gas stove in the motor home, he'd heated several strips of freeze-dried bacon, scrambled some powdered eggs, and percolated fresh coffee. He would never have imagined that he'd ever care for powdered eggs, but he observed somewhat wryly that one's standards tend to drop with extended abstinence from the real thing.

He had given a lot of thought to trying to stretch the canned ground coffee over several years, but he knew that it would turn stale within months, so he might as well enjoy it while it was fresh. He still had over a hundred pounds of coffee beans as well as a small hand-grinder. He'd sealed the bags of beans in a plastic trash bag along with a desiccant, planning to keep the coffee relatively fresh for as long as possible.

CC trudged through the trees, heading south around the end of the canyon. Crossing a small meadow, he reached the wood road up which he'd originally driven the truck. There was a large pile of old used lumber rotting beside the road. The remains of a stone foundation were collapsing into a cellar that was overgrown with weeds, and he suspected that the stack of rotting lumber had come from the house that had once stood there. Yellow jackets buzzed lackadaisically around the pile of boards, and his movements disturbed a robin tugging at a worm beside the road. The air was very clear, and everything seemed larger than life.

He continued up the road toward the extreme west end of the canyon. A little beyond the ruined farm, he was faced with a choice. The wood road itself headed on toward the cliffs at the end of the valley, but a lane turned off to the left, toward the long south wall of the canyon. He opted to continue on west toward the end of the valley, eager to discover the source of the stream. His journey ended at the base of a cliff.

Instead of discovering the source of the stream, he was surprised to find a long earth ramp which entered another cave that opened about twenty feet above the valley floor. A large concrete portal had been built at the mouth of the cave to reinforce the entrance. Two huge, deeply weathered and ancient brick chimneys — probably kilns for heating the limestone — were built at the base of the cliff next to the portal. Their positioning would have made it easy to charge them with lime and charcoal from above and to remove the cement from below.

CC wandered over to study them more closely. The old mortar was flaking from the joints, and when he ran his finger along a seam, it turned to dust and fell from the crack. It was pretty obvious that the bricks had been set in a mixture of lime and local sand many years before. A concrete slab had been poured beneath the front of the firebox at the base of one kiln.

He kicked a rusted can from its overgrown surface, and noticed some letters scratched in the surface of the concrete. Kneeling, he brushed aside the dirt. Someone had inscribed his initials, "J.S.," and the year. CC wondered what had happened to J.S., and pondered how many decades had passed since these cement kilns had last been fired.

The Kiln, the Bridge, and the Farm

West end of Hidden Valley

May 21st, 9:15 a.m.

He was enjoying the sunshine, and had no desire to enter this newly discovered cave, so he turned to follow a rugged path that ran parallel to the base of the cliff at the west end of the valley. He followed it through heavy brush and up and down over rocky ground, and he had to stop twice to pull burdock from his trouser legs. He expected to find the headwaters of the creek soon, and kept looking up at the cliffs, hoping to spot a waterfall or some other evidence of its source.

Walking slowly over the rough terrain he finally came to a large pond at the base of the cliff. The surface was agitated, and CC realized that it was probably fed by an underground source. Instead of continuing on around the pond, he turned back and walked around its south side. When he reached the stream at the east end, he followed it toward the valley's entrance, well over a half mile away. After walking about fifty yards, he turned back to examine the base of the cliff.

At the far end of the pond, he noticed a dark hole in the rock that rose just above the surface of the water and realized that it was probably a submerged cave. It seemed probable that the stream flowed out of the mountain through an underground cavern, then collected in this pond before flowing down the center of the valley. He spotted the opening of another cave, just off to the side of the first, but above water level.

CC realized that he wouldn't have been able to spot the top of the submerged cave if the water in the stream bed had not dropped over the past few days. He continued walking east, making his way downstream toward the bottleneck which was still over a half mile away. The stream's banks now rose sharply on both sides, effectively hiding him from anyone who might be moving about the valley floor.

A couple of hundred yards downstream a bridge crossed the stream. When he scrambled up the embankment, he realized that he was standing on the lane that he'd passed a few minutes earlier. He decided to cross the bridge and continue toward the south wall of the valley.

He paused. There seemed something strange and out of place about the bridge, but he couldn't readily identify it, but just being near it made him feel uncomfortable and exposed. He sat down on a rock below the edge of the embankment and examined the structure. He stared at it for several minutes before he realized what was odd about it.

The wooden beams which supported it were pale green, pressure-treated lumber that had lightened only slightly with age. This bridge was almost new! He noted that its limestone abutments had been carefully dressed and laid up, and that there were freshly poured footings at both ends.

Moving down the bank to examine the closest footing, he noticed the initials, "J.S." scratched into the masonry, along with the previous year's date. *This was a man who obviously took pride in his work, but a man who had to be at least seventy years old.* The construction of this bridge would be an impressive achievement even for a young man. Then a worrisome thought struck. *I wonder whether J.S. is, or was, a recluse?*

He continued to study the well-designed structure for
several minutes, lost in the questions that enfiladed his mind.
His confidence was shaken.

*If this bridge was built in the past year, it's obvious that this valley
is not abandoned. Or at least it wasn't before the war began. Has J.S.
also been seeking seclusion? Since before the war? It certainly seems so, for
he's left the entry to the valley in a primitive condition. But even if he
proves friendly, the valley will not be a safe place for me, because someone
outside must know of his presence here.* And then CC's thinking
took another tact. *Suppose he shoots first, and ask questions later.*

That thought shattered any illusion of security he had
begun to enjoy, leaving him stunned. He sat there for several
minutes longer. A little rest would do him no harm, and it
might give his churning thoughts time to jell. He lifted his
head so that he could see above the top of the stream bank so
that he could survey the valley around him. There seemed to
be no movement anywhere in the vicinity, so he stood and
made his way to the north end of the bridge. It was a one-
lane structure with a wooden deck, maybe forty feet long, and
just wide enough to take a car or farm tractor. It didn't so
much as vibrate under his weight.

He crossed the bridge, and stopped to gaze up the lane.
It was obvious that it had not been traveled in some time, as
there were weeds growing in the wheel ruts. Small meadows
lay to either side of the road. They were separated by
windrows of tall trees and tumbled stone walls. He continued
south toward a stand of tall pines that seemed to fill the entire
southwest corner of the valley. It occurred to him that Black
River Junction lay about thirty miles beyond the canyon's
north wall.

CC was surprised to see that the road he was following
meandered back and forth, keeping to the more difficult terrain, winding beneath the branches of the larger trees and
alongside steep rocky outcroppings. As he trudged along the
road, the high weeds dragged at his legs, and the grass, shiny
with dew, soaked his shoes.

He followed the lane as it curved around a knoll on his left, then reversed itself to continue toward the cliffs. He went on for perhaps a hundred paces, and entered the pines. The tall evergreens now bordered both sides of the narrow lane. The lower branches that bordered the lane had been cut back to allow passage, but he was still unable to see through the thick growth on either side. The boughs were so thick that he could not see the cliffs that loomed behind them.

He became increasingly nervous, and was careful to avoid stepping on sticks or dry leaves that might crackle under his feet. Suddenly the track narrowed, and though it continued on, it was overgrown and beyond this point was rarely traveled. That didn't make sense to him. He stopped and began searching the shadows beneath the huge evergreens. The wheel ruts in the lane he'd followed had petered out when he'd reached rockier soil, and now there were no wheel tracks whatever. He wondered where the vehicles had exited the lane.

The two trees on his immediate right seemed to be missing a few of their lower branches. When he peered into the shadows beneath those trees, he noticed several very small evergreens growing between them, their trunks heaped with dried brown needles. Between the lane on which he stood, and those small pines on his right, he noticed two parallel tire tracks that ran right up to and disappeared beneath those small pines.

The Farmhouse

Southwest Corner of the Valley

May 21st, 10:25 a.m.

CC stared down at the tire tracks, then bent down to walk beneath the low branches, kicking aside the deep piles of pine needles that were heaped around the trunks of the smaller trees. The mystery was solved. Those three little evergreens were being grown in shallow wooden tubs, and the tubs had been heaped around with pine needles to disguise them and obscure whatever lay beyond.

The branches above his head had been bruised, presumably by a vehicle passing beneath them. CC moved on. It was obvious that someone had gone to a lot of trouble to hide this path, but had slipped up the last time they'd used it.

CC didn't have to let his imagination go far afield to realize that he might very well be trespassing on some misanthrope who would delight in killing him and burying his body in a remote corner of this lonely canyon. His curiosity got the better of him, and he continued on. After about ten yards, the pines thinned out, and he could make out the canyon wall in the near distance. Standing just within the cover of the large trees, he studied the scene that was now opened up to him.

The sheer rock escarpment sloped up and out toward him, overhanging the valley below and forming an enormous hollow that seemed to embrace the ground below, like a vast band shell. In the shelter of this depression were nestled two buildings.

To his left, about one hundred feet out from the cliff, stood a rustic cottage. Slightly behind the cottage, and to its right, stood a barn. Both buildings were clean of line and beautifully maintained. They were constructed of rough-sawn lumber in the board-and-batten style, the roofs shingled with well-weathered cedar shakes, their walls stained a rich cocoa.

As he crept forward, he could see that everything about the place — from the lush ivy that climbed the massive field-stone chimney, to the roses that lined the neatly laid granite walks — had received loving care. A large fenced vegetable garden lay well out from the cliff where it would enjoy long hours of sunlight. A pasture enclosed with woven wire fencing occupied most of the area overhung by the towering concave cliff, providing livestock, which were not in evidence, with a grazing area that would be protected from the worst of the summer sun and winter blast. The little farm had a fairy-tale quality, and he blinked his eyes as he examined the house to make certain it wasn't constructed of gingerbread and candy drops.

In spite of the warm day, CC noticed that the temperature dropped appreciably as he neared the cliffs. He reasoned that the massive overhang would protect much of the area from the summer sun, while the dark cliffs would radiate a pleasant chill. In winter the process would probably be reversed. The sun, hanging low in the southeastern sky, would light the hollow for the early part of the day, warming its inhabitants and heating the concave surface of the huge rock wall. And at night that rocky mass would radiate back any warmth it had absorbed during the day. He grunted in appreciation.

Solar heating and cooling on a massive scale, and it didn't cost a penny more to locate the buildings here than anywhere else in the valley. This is one very smart man!

Standing in the shadows under one of the trees, he studied the setting carefully. He had stopped behind a trellis covered with climbing roses that was adjacent to the garden. Seedlings had been planted in careful rows, but were now threatened by encroaching weeds. A forty-year-old pickup truck sat beside the house, the driver's door open. These things contradicted the meticulous appearance of the place, and struck a warning chord that everything might not be as it seemed in this otherwise idyllic pastoral scene.

The very beauty of the homestead seemed to argue against a tenant of perverse character. This was obviously a product of creative people who worked the soil and loved beauty and order. CC sensed that he had nothing to fear here, though he knew that some of the most evil people in world history had also cherished beauty and order.

He moved beneath a large tree from which he could better view the house while remaining hidden, hoping for some movement, some sign of life. He'd begun to realize that, although he was afraid of contact with others, he was also starved for human fellowship.

Well, I've got one foot in the water; might as well dive right in. And he started boldly for the front door. He strode up the flag pathway, the dark stone slabs dramatically accented by a tumult of colorful petunias and geraniums bordering the walk. Lush grass grew several inches high between the stepping stones. The flowers were a visual delight, but he reasoned that they were a woman's touch, for a man would almost certainly have to devote all of his energies to support this isolated farm, and would not have time to concern himself with what he might be considered a frivolous and time-consuming hobby.

Then he caught himself laughing aloud, mocking his own thoughts. While the male of the species had historically been preoccupied with what he considered the weightier matters of life, the women, no matter how overworked, had always seemed to find a way to satisfy a natural passion for the things that enriched the world. A few months ago, his politically incorrect thoughts would have seen him branded as sexist, but he could not withdraw from his conviction that women were truly the fairer sex in every sense.

As he neared the house, he could see that the bright red shutters were thrown wide to welcome light through large window panes. The shutters were not merely decorative but obviously designed to be closed in bad weather. Roses grew along the front of the house in magnificent profusion. He could see that there were white lace curtains hanging in the windows. A large flat rock served as a doorstep.

Man's Best Friend

Inside the Farm House
May 21th, 11:10 a.m.

CC stood on the front step of the cottage, staring at the screen door. There were smears of dried mud and claw marks along the door frame, evidence that an animal had attempted to get into the house. He peered through the screen door. The house door stood open a few inches, and from the mud on the floor, he realized that the animal had succeeded in getting inside.

The screen door opened smoothly, and he smiled at the incongruity of a bright red front door, with its large shiny brass knocker, in the midst of this seeming wilderness. *That seems to indicate that they might welcome visitors,* he concluded.

He grasped the knocker and tapped it tentatively against its brass seat. When there was no response, he raised it higher and struck it more forcefully. The resulting noise unnerved him, and he stumbled back against the screen door, half expecting someone to come storming out at him.

Gotta get control of myself, he thought. When there was no response to the racket he'd made, he turned to search the woods, aware of the possibility that, even in this isolated place, he might be stalked.

When he turned back to the door, he still hesitated to enter. Even now, in a world ravaged by war, he shrank from breaking the taboo against entering another man's home uninvited. He walked slowly around to the back of the house, and stepped up on a small deck. There was a glass storm-door that would give access to the rear of the house. When he tried the handle, he found it locked. Curtains obscured any view of the interior.

He began to think that he'd been alone for too long, for he was reading ominous signs into everything he saw. In spite of his determination to exercise a positive attitude, the silence seemed sinister to him. He looked for any sign of activity, any evidence of life. There were no clothes on the line, and when he looked up at the chimney, there was no smoke.

Returning to the front door, he pushed the handle and found the door opening smoothly. He stopped abruptly when he heard a weak voice, interrupted by the threatening growl of a dog. CC shaped the word, "Hello?" as a question, and received a muted snarl in response.

The voice he had heard seemed to come from an adjoining room, and he thought he could hear the dog scrabble to its feet, so he braced himself for an attack.

Turning to escape, he noticed that there was dried mud on the inside of the front door as well, and wondered if the animal had tried to close it. It wasn't unusual to find a dog with the intelligence to let himself in and out of a door that was left partially open, or to even turn a knob with his teeth.

He stepped back against the screen door and heard the latch click as it seated itself, leaving him between the closed screen and the partially open main door, and evoking the image of raking claws and slavering fangs. By the time he'd re-opened the screen door, the growling had subsided, and CC heard only a low whine. A man's voice continued monotonously in the background, as though he were insensitive or indifferent to the dog's warning growl.

It was cold in the house, and a room which would ordinarily appear cheerful now seemed to possess a gaudy unfriendliness, exhaling an unhealthy flatulence. CC recognized it. It was the now too familiar sickening-sweet odor of death that permeated the atmosphere.

He looked around him. It would, under other circumstances, be a very comfortable room. A rugged stone fireplace occupied the center of the end wall, and he took note of the cold gray ashes heaped around the andirons. The room contained a pine trestle table with a clear finish, matching chairs and china cupboard, a desk, with a loose-cushioned chintz sofa, and two matching easy chairs arranged in front of the fireplace. There was a kerosene lamp in the center of the table, and an entire wall of floor-to-ceiling shelves, packed with books.

At the opposite end of the large room was an attractive and efficient little kitchen, complete with sink and old-fashioned hand pump. Alongside the pump were contemporary hot and cold water faucets. There was a bank of knotty pine cabinets, a refrigerator, and a wood stove. A refrigerator?

In the light that seeped through the curtains CC could make out two unlit electric light fixtures hanging from the ceiling. He went to the front window to look out over the yard. He could see no utility poles. He turned to stare again at the refrigerator. Through the bathroom door, he could see light reflected off the surfaces of several porcelain fixtures.

He realized that the growling he'd heard had been coming from another door. He took an afghan from the sofa — an intricately-crocheted comforter — and wrapped it around his left arm. Then he picked up a poker from beside the fireplace, and moved toward the door. He didn't want to hurt the dog if he didn't have to, but he had no intention of suffering harm if it was avoidable.

CC knocked on the door. "Hello. Is there anyone in there?"

Receiving another growl in response, he braced his shoulder against the casing and pushed the door open, inch by careful inch. He gripped the door knob and prepared to yank it closed if the dog attempted to attack him. The dog's growl instead subsided to a whimper, and the scrabbling sound ceased. CC worked his hand more firmly around the poker handle and pushed the door open far enough to peer around its frame.

The cloying odor of death was overwhelming, and he gagged. He dropped the poker and ran through the house to the bathroom where he knelt before the toilet, racked with sickness. After a while, he rinsed his mouth and washed his face. It was only after he'd turned off the lavatory faucet that it registered on him that there was substantial water pressure, but he did not pause to consider the significance of this phenomenon. Instead, he steeled himself to reenter the room. This time he put on a surgical mask, and, having learned from experience, sprinkled a couple of drops of fragrant aftershave on it. It would not overcome the smell, but it might help mask it.

He slipped into the room, and as his eyes adjusted to the gloom, he saw a dog lying at the foot of the bed, obviously too ill or weak to move. Then CC saw a figure lying on the bed. The voice he thought he'd heard was now replaced by dissonant music. It was coming from a small portable radio on a night stand. He realized that he'd again been fooled by a radio.

The music faded in and out, and he wondered how many radios in the world were leaching the last of the power from their batteries.

But what kind of batteries, he wondered, *would keep that radio operating for an entire month?*

He listened closely, pondering who could be broadcasting, and what they were using for power. The answer was quick in coming. An announcer identified the station as "The Voice of New England," representing the liberating forces of Asia, and "bringing a new wind of social, economic, and political responsibility to America."

Uttering soft assurances to the dog, CC stepped carefully around him to shut off the radio. He did a double take. It was not battery-powered, but plugged into an electrical outlet. In this valley, at least, the power was still on. *That explains the refrigerator and the water pressure,* he concluded.

The dog lifted his head to watch CC move by him, then dropped his chin onto his paws and ceased his whining, but his head rolled slowly from side to side as his eyes followed CC's every move.

CC turned to the window and opened the drapes. As he turned back toward the bed, he got a clearer look at the corpse. Laying there were the remains of a leathery old man, his bedclothes stained with dried blood and vomit, evidence of his losing battle with radiation poisoning.

CC opened the window to clear the air, then left the room. Out of habit, he checked the sensor he kept pinned to his lapel, and was reassured to see that he had received no cumulative rads, and that there was no evidence of residual radiation remaining in the house. If radioactivity killed this old man, he had probably been exposed to it while outside during the worst of the fallout.

According to one book CC had read as he waited out his two weeks in the X-ray room, radiation affects different organisms in different ways. Human beings are the first to be impacted, and die most quickly; animals next; then plants and trees; followed by insects. Ironically, the insects which have plagued the race since Adam and Eve were evicted from the Garden are able to survive the longest. Perhaps not ironically, the deadliest organisms, such as viruses, are most resistant to one of man's most horrible weapons.

In spite of the fact that CC believed in life after death, he somehow knew that he'd always had difficulty dealing with its trappings — undertakers, mortuaries, and cemeteries. And even though he had recently become familiar with death in many guises, he had not become inured to its horror or to its seeming finality.

He thought, *When a man breathes his last, his option to receive Jesus Christ as his Savior passes with him.*

Each time that he was exposed to it, he felt less able to cope. His spiritual strength seemed to ebb, and he felt something of himself slip away. Instinctively he found himself identifying with the sufferers, and a little more life seemed to be squeezed out of him with each death observed.

That's why the valley means so much to me, he thought. *It's a place where I'd hoped I'd finally escaped the horror, and might ultimately be healed, but here I am, standing next to this old man's remains.*

He realized that he was weeping and he gave himself over to his grief. Sliding to his knees, he allowed the wracking sobs to have their way with him. *Perhaps,* he thought, *they might wash something of the horror away.* And indeed the tears did seem to flush the poison from his system. As he wiped them from his face, he felt used up, but somehow cleaner. He reasoned that if he was still able to feel awful sorrow in the face of death, then he was undoubtedly healthier than those who had become inured to it and were unable to cry.

He stumbled toward the kitchen, his vision blurred. Ducking his head beneath the faucet, he splashed cold water over his face, then pushed his head under the frigid stream. After a moment, he turned his face to the faucet and drank. The icy liquid tasted wonderful to his parched mouth and throat. He found a clean towel in a cabinet, and rubbed his hair and face dry.

He felt something brush his knee and looked down to discover the dog looking up at him as though sharing his grief. The animal slowly lifted his paw to CC's leg, probably as starved for companionship as for food. One thing seemed certain, he exemplified the species' reputation for loyalty. He had made his way into the house to share the final days of his master's life and had never left his side.

How then, had he survived? CC wondered. The answer wasn't long in coming. He noticed an open pantry door, and peering inside, he could see the teeth and claw marks where the dog had ripped open a large bag of dried dog food. The bag was empty, every bit of the food gone. Near the sink was a drinking bowl, long since emptied, but when CC stuck his head into the bathroom, he saw that someone had evidently filled the bathtub with water, and it seemed obvious that the dog had survived on it, for there was only a cup or two of soiled water near the drain plug.

CC reached down gently and took the dog's muzzle between his hands, caressing him and scratching his neck. The dog made a throaty little whine, closed his eyes with pleasure, then opened them again as if to make certain he wasn't going too far in trusting a stranger. CC knelt down and bundled the dog in his arms. Under the thick fur, he was emaciated and no burden to lift.

He carried him to the dining area, and laid him gently on a rug. There were two large dishes on the floor in the kitchen. No telling how long since the dog had finished up whatever food and water was there. He searched through the cabinets for something to feed him. He found a case of dog food, opened a can, and placed half of it in a clean bowl. The dog sniffed at the food, licked it, and lay down again.

He coaxed the animal. "Come on, boy. You have to eat."

The dog rolled his eyes toward him and whined.

"Come on, now." CC spoke firmly, insistently. "Eat!"

The animal looked at him, seemed to sigh, tipped his mouth to the plate, and took a tentative bite. He swallowed it with some difficulty, but with the tasting, seemed to gain appetite. He wolfed the rest down in two bites and looked to CC for more.

"No, boy. Too much food all at once will make you sick." He picked up the plate, and put it in the sink. "I'll give you more later," he assured the animal.

The dog struggled to his feet, moved to an oval rug in the corner, followed his tail in a circle, flopped down, and rested his jowls on his paws, his eyes never ceasing to follow CC's every movement.

CC looked back toward the bedroom. He realized that he should get out and leave everything as it was so that any other intruders would believe that this was the end of life in this valley, but he reasoned that it wouldn't be right. He couldn't bury all of America's dead, but this one was given him to do. Nor, he realized, would leaving the corpse here promote his own privacy, for the next visitors would probably assume it was a safe place for them to hide as well.

He found himself staring at the old man, trying to read the riddle of his life. Evidently, gamma sterilization had slowed decay, even as, before the war, it had been increasingly used by food processing companies for food preservation.

Even in pale death he had great dignity. He was about 70, of medium height, lean, almost stringy. He wore the rough, warm clothes of the woodsman-farmer, a heavy plaid wool shirt, rugged brown canvas trousers, high leather boots with rubberized soles, and wool socks rolled down over the tops.

He had closed his eyes in death. They were set in deep sockets, and gave his ascetic face an appearance of intense gravity and intelligence. Yet the crow's feet about his eyes gave lie to any appearance of gloom. His hands were callused, but the fingers were long and finely-shaped, like those of a musician or an artist. His high forehead was crowned with a shock of brown hair, run through with gray.

CC thought aloud, "This was a man of worth." He shook his head. "I can't leave his remains laying here."

Nonetheless, he realized that his first responsibility was to the living. He filled a clean bowl with fresh water and took it to the dog. At first the animal just lay there, staring dumbly at him, but CC scratched behind his ears, and spoke encouragingly to him in a quiet voice. The dog got to his feet, lowered his head, and began to lap noisily, but when CC offered him the other half can of food, he simply stared at it and went to sleep.

CC was glad he'd found the dog food. He would have to be careful to feed the dog only canned goods that he'd checked for radiation. He'd been extremely careful to avoid ingesting radioactive materials through the food chain. Doing so would result in cancer and an agonizing death. He wondered why the dog had not succumbed to the radiation. Perhaps he didn't enter the house until after the radiation had lost its power, but, if so, where had he been hiding?

"Ashes to Ashes"

Between the Farm House and the Cliff

May 21st, 2:25 p.m.

CC found a pick, shovel, and leather work gloves in the barn, and carried them over to a small shaded knoll that lay midway between the house and the cliff.

His chest still bothered him on occasion, and he didn't look forward to any hard digging, but as it turned out, it wasn't required. The soil proved to be quite sandy and he was able to manage his pain while he dug the shallow grave. The dark chore, however, did nothing to help drive away his personal sense of loss and depression.

When he returned to the house, he saw that the dog had eaten the remainder of the food in his bowl and was again asleep. CC patted his shoulder and the animal opened one eye, then scrambled to his feet to follow CC into the bedroom. He tried to climb up on the bed, but lacked the strength, so CC lifted his wasted body onto the edge, and the dog crept over to lie next to the old man. The dog avoided touching the body, but lay on his stomach, his paws stretched out before him, whining thinly.

The dog looks like he's praying, CC thought, and imagined he could see tears in his eyes. He was surprised at the concern he felt for the dog, and realized that he was probably as starved for companionship as was the animal.

"Okay, fella. It's time to say, 'good-bye.'" The dog seemed to understand, for he whimpered one last time, slid back onto his hind legs, and allowed CC to lower him to the floor. He stood on his hind feet to look out the window, his tail noticeably immobile, pointedly ignoring CC's activities as he prepared his former master's body for its final rest.

Starting at each corner of the bed, CC reached down and pulled the covers loose, then threw the corners diagonally across the body, enclosing it in a cocoon of blankets. Wearing gloves, he tied rough knots in the bedding, then carefully rolled the remains onto a piece of canvas he'd found in the barn, wrapping it tightly. Sliding the bundle to the floor, he tied it atop a wide plank.

Lifting one end of the plank, he dragged it carefully out the back door and across the little deck. It was hard work, and he was perspiring and breathing hard by the time he reached the grave.

The dog began to whine again. Taking one fold of the canvas between his teeth, he sat back on his haunches, resisting CC's efforts to move the body any nearer the grave. CC took exaggerated care in gently setting down his burden. Then he knelt beside the dog and spoke soberly to him of the sorrowful end of all life in this world. He knew the dog could not comprehend his words, but he was sure the creature understood the tears in his eyes and could sense the respect that CC had for his master's remains.

He kept the body fastened to the plank, but getting it down into the grave without dropping it was tricky. At one point, he lost control, and the body pitched headlong to the bottom of the shallow grave. CC stared down into the hole, heart-struck.

Sure, millions of people had been cast into graves through the centuries. And right now, millions lay decomposing wherever they had been struck down, but for some reason it bothered him to think that this particular man's sightless eyes would be forever staring symbolically toward the bowels of the earth, instead of upward toward light and air and God. It was irrational, he knew. After all, these were simply his earthly remains. The soul which had been breathed into him had already passed into the Lord's presence.

Apart from emotional concerns, it would be dangerous for CC to try to lower himself down into that grave again, but he did. And somehow he managed to get a rope under the board to which the body was fastened, to climb back out, and twist and pull on that rope until he got it into an acceptable position. It took quite a while, and he was completely exhausted and soaked with sweat when he'd finished.

In spite of that, he felt compelled to say some words over the grave. They flowed far more freely than a layman might expect, and he found himself quoting Jesus: "In my Father's house are many mansions.... I go there to prepare a place for you." And he remembered Paul's glorious rhetorical question, "Death, where is thy victory? Grave, where is thy sting?" And after he uttered them, he was surprised and oddly gratified that they had sprung spontaneously from somewhere deep within him.

He shoveled the earth slowly into the grave, while tears, for the third time that day, ran from his eyes. The dog lay there the entire time, his muzzle on his paws, eyes unblinking as he watched CC's every motion. He moved only once, to turn away from the grave. Then, to CC's amazement, he used his two hind feet to kick a little loose dirt into the hole. After that, he drew apart, his eyes following each shovel of earth as CC lifted it from the pile and dropped it into the grave.

The dog scrabbled to his feet and came to CC's side. For the moment, they seemed partners in sorrow. The dog shook himself, as though relinquishing his former life, then licked CC's hand, adopting a new friend and master from among the living. CC wished that he could shake himself too, and start over so easily.

As tired as he was, he transplanted a small rose bush from the front of the house to the head of the grave. When he was finished, he walked slowly to the barn, and, as he was hanging the tools up, noticed a tool box with the initials J.S. stenciled on top.

The man I just buried must be J.S., he thought. So I've found the man who poured the concrete slab beneath that cement kiln decades ago, the man who had engineered that ingenious bridge across the stream, and who built this homestead.

CC rummaged through the box for a saw and a hammer, and assembled a crude cross from some scrap lumber. He found a can of white spray paint, and quickly painted it. Then he walked back to the burial plot, pushed the point into the soft earth, and stood at attention for a moment, refusing to cry any more. Then he turned back to the house, the dog following closely at his heels.

His work was still unfinished. He put on some rubber gloves and used a garden rake to drag the mattress out to a remote area beneath the cliff. He found a can of gasoline in the barn, and splashed a little on the mattress, then set fire to the bedding. The heat was so intense that it gave off almost no smoke, nor did he believe that the flames would be seen in bright daylight.

He returned to the house and scrubbed the bedroom floor with disinfectant. He was filthy from his labors, and he braced himself for an icy shock as he stepped under the shower. It was a shock all right, but not an icy one. There was plenty of hot water! Another riddle. In spite of the wonder of this unexpected luxury, however, CC could not wash away the memory of this day's dark labors.

It was early evening, but CC didn't feel like eating. After digging the grave, he'd scraped the grit from beneath his fingernails, but he still felt somehow soiled. And he had a nervous stomach. He realized that he couldn't cross the valley and get back to his cave before dark, and he was too tired to make the effort. Nor could he bring himself to spend the night in the house, especially since he had no idea what or who was behind the one remaining unopened door. That would have to wait for the morrow. So he found a couple of fresh blankets in a plastic bag on the linen closet shelf, and carried them out to the hayloft in the barn.

There was something wonderfully restful about this pastoral scene — the old post and beam construction of the barn, the hay for the domestic animals, and the persistent pursuit of life by all creatures, great and small. The odor of the hay, the motes floating in the last rays of the setting sun, the chirp of a cricket, a honeybee making its last sojourn of the day, and the busied frenzy of a barn-swallow feeding her young — all these helped the day's grisly labor to fade. As the chill of the spring night began to penetrate the barn, CC burrowed a little deeper into the hay and finally fell into a healing sleep.

Another Enigma

The Barn

May 22nd, 7:40 a.m.

Hours later, the sun splashed over the barn, pouring through every chance opening, drenching him with the warm sweet light of a new day. He awoke feeling better than at any time since he'd entered this new life of forced anonymity. And he was hungry.

He climbed down the ladder from the loft. The dog, without his being aware of it, had followed him to the barn, and had curled up in a heap of hay near the base of the ladder. Now he followed CC back to the house.

CC fed him another can of the dog food, then rummaged through the refrigerator. He discovered a side of bacon, a can of coffee, and some eggs in the refrigerator, and a loaf of homemade bread in the freezer. He discarded the old eggs, brewed a pot of coffee, fried a half-dozen slices of the bacon, toasted four slices of the bread, and spread it with real butter to make bacon sandwiches. He enjoyed the breakfast immensely as he sat on the doorstep and looked over the farm.

Taking one of the bacon sandwiches in one hand, and his coffee cup in the other, he walked twice around the house looking for the electrical entry system. There was none. No overhead wires. No transformer. No electrical meter box. No circuit breaker box. Nor was there a windmill or any solar panels. All he found was a waterproof cable that came up out of the ground and entered the house through a service head. In an inside closet, he found a small circuit breaker box. He was puzzled. Though he'd found the supply line, it didn't account for the fact that the household appliances worked. And from where did that line draw its current?

There were three power distribution grids in America — the eastern U.S., the western U.S., and Texas.

Leave it to the Texans, he smiled. *They probably still have power, but as for the rest of America, the production and distribution of electricity has probably ceased. Obviously power is out throughout the northeast corridor. Therefore the refrigerator in this house simply cannot work. Nor can the toaster, the coffee percolator, or the range. Yet, they do!*

It would be understating the case to say that he was excited about his discovery. In the past, electricity had powered almost every convenience and labor-saving device in America. It had driven America's industries, lighted its stores, refrigerated its food, and energized its computers. Yet he realized that he may have discovered an independent source of power right here in this remote valley.

A Subterranean Stable

The Cliffs Behind the Barn
May 22nd, about 8:30 a.m.

CC decided to let the dog tag along as he did some exploring. The dog looked part Lab and part Shepherd, entirely black except for a blaze of white at his throat. As CC started back down the path toward the barn, he called, "Come on, Blacky." Whatever his real name, the dog seemed satisfied with the one CC had just given him, and stood to his feet to follow.

The barn proved to be beautifully cared for. It was clean, well-repaired, and extraordinarily well-organized. CC spent a half hour exploring its secrets. It was larger than he had at first assumed. There was a small, well-equipped workshop, tack room, stanchions for four cows, empty stalls for livestock and horses, a small tractor, assorted farm implements, and a large quantity of hay and grain.

There was also a full corn crib, and even a stack of salt blocks. The poultry yard was small, but modern, as was the pigpen, which had a concrete floor and was not the typical filthy wallow. *Yet neither swine, nor fowl, nor bovine do I see,* he thought, and wondered what had become of them.

As he walked out toward the corral, the dog tried to anticipate his movements, skittering back and forth like a leaf on a windy fall day. He would alternately brush against CC, then dash out in front to lead the way, barking with excitement. The fenced pasture ran up to the overhanging mountain wall, and the irregular lay of the fence line beneath the scattered trees served to hide the farm from the air.

As he neared the cliff, CC kept an eye out for snakes, but when the dog ran ahead toward the base of the escarpment, he relaxed a little, reasonably sure that the dog would warn him of any danger. CC called to him to come back, but the canine disappeared into a heavy growth of cedars that hid the base of the cliff. When he reached the trees, he realized that the dog was following a well-worn path around the back of the evergreens.

Just behind the trees, he found a five-hundred gallon tank with a hand-crank pump on top, and a small farm tractor parked next to it. He unscrewed a cap from the top of the tank and peered into it. It was about half full of gasoline. What a discovery!

A narrow trail wound between the base of the overhanging cliff and the trees. It turned sharply right, and CC found himself peering into a tall vertical opening in the cliff wall. On either side of this opening rested huge slabs of rock, overgrown with vines, criss-crossing in the dusk high above him, forming a roof-like entrance to a natural cave. The cave had been invisible from the farm because it entered the cliff at a sharp angle, like the oblique slash of an ax in a log. The worn path and aging animal droppings seemed to indicate that farm animals had frequently moved in and out.

CC stepped cautiously beneath the shadow of the rocks. Just inside the entrance he found a shelf that held a couple of kerosene lanterns, a can of fuel, and a Ball jar filled with wood matches. He lit one of the lanterns and followed the excited dog into the narrow twisting cave. The roof dropped abruptly until it was just a few feet above his head, then narrowed so that he could easily reach out and touch both walls. The dog had disappeared, but his barks echoed back down the tunnel.

The dank odor of the cave changed, sharpened by the acrid smell of urine. CC turned a corner and was faced with an astonishing sight. The dog was scampering about before a wide Dutch door made of heavy timbers that closed off the tunnel. Peering over this door, CC could see a low-wattage light bulb burning dully in a fixture on the cave wall.

He opened the gate and entered an underground room that was larger than the one in which he'd parked the tractor-trailer. In the intense glow of the lantern's glare, he could see dozens of farm animals roaming about, some moving toward him, their various voices setting up a raucous demonstration of excitement, complaint and petition.

CC stood transfixed. The dog had led him to a farmer's most precious of possessions — his livestock. This small assortment of creatures was a remarkable find in a world where countless domestic animals had been destroyed by war and neglect. He pushed the gate closed to keep the animals in, and moved on for a more careful inspection.

Apart from a sow and her litter of pigs, there were several goats, a number of sheep, a flock of chickens, another of turkeys, ducks, even a gaggle of geese. Most importantly, he counted one milk cow and two horses. Horses? Draught animals! Creatures that could move heavy burdens but would not require a supply of gasoline or replacement parts. *This is one*

of the great discoveries of my brief post-war experience. Then he cor-
rected himself. *This war is far from over.*

He walked slowly toward one of the horses. The animal
stretched out his neck to snuffle at his outstretched hand.
When he began to withdraw in disappointment at not receiving a treat, CC moved in to rub the mare's jaws between his
hands, then patted her gently on the neck. She responded by
gently laying her head on his shoulder. After a moment, CC
moved away from the horse to take in more of the scene.

The old man had obviously been a good farmer, a man
who cared for his stock. He had arranged things so that water
flowed in through a pipe at the upper end of the room,
formed a pool at the center where the animals could drink,
then ran toward the tunnel where it dropped into a grating
and was evidently carried away through another tunnel.

In the center of the room was a basket-like device made
of flat iron, perhaps eight feet in diameter and as many feet
high, where hay had been stacked for the livestock. It was
empty now, except for a few random stems of grass rotting in
the mud beneath, but there were hay bales stacked in a corner, and although the animals had ripped them open and ruined much of the hay by dragging it through the muck, they'd
clearly had sufficient to eat.

Along the back wall there were several large, rat-proof
steel bins. When CC lifted the lids, he found that they were
filled with seed — wheat, rye, oats, and corn — as well as one
filled with poultry feed. He thought it strange that there were
a couple of steel tool boxes stacked on the seed bins until he
opened them and discovered they were filled with packets of
native fruit and vegetable seeds packaged in plastic bags and
carefully labeled. It was immediately clear that these were not
hybrids or genetically engineered, but were heritage seeds, native stock that would pollinate to produce healthy fruit and
vegetables.

The poultry feeders were nearly full, and while he wasn't
a farmer, this tested his credulity. He found mash in several

garbage cans, threw some in the dry corner where there were roosts for the chickens, then topped off the feeders. No point freeing the animals, he thought, until he knew what he wanted to do with them. For the time being they seemed much safer in here than out in the open.

He was no farmer, but he knew that the animals couldn't wait a prolonged period while he studied the subject. On the other hand, he dared not make any mistakes. And if anyone discovered them, they would be more apt to slaughter them for food than to recognize their potential for reproduction. No thought process was required in concluding that the livestock had belonged to the man he'd recently laid to rest, and were therefore now his responsibility.

Having seen to his new menagerie's appetites, he used a shovel to push some of the manure into a compost pile, then looked up once more to survey the room. The light from his lantern fell upon some words on the wall, and he stepped closer to read them. With a piece of charcoal, someone had scratched the words, "Joseph's Ark." CC now knew the farmer's first name, and that someone possessed a sense of humor.

There was a wooden tack chest on the ground near the Dutch door, and several bridles and harness sets hung from dowels set in holes drilled into the rock. CC opened the chest and found a saddle and a variety of tools — among them curry combs, brushes, liniment, and blankets. He was most intrigued with a couple of hard hats that had miner's lanterns fastened to their fronts. Beside them he found several tightly sealed jars containing little pieces of gravel labeled "calcium carbide."

Most high school chemistry students learn that when calcium carbide is immersed in water, it generates acetylene gas, but CC didn't have the least notion of how much of the mineral to put in the lantern's generator tank, nor how much water to pour in with it. So he poured about a tablespoon of the granules into the reservoir, filled it half full of clear spring water, screwed the cap back on, and reached into the concave reflector to spin the serrated wheel against the flint. The spark ignited a jet of invisible gas, creating a long, pencil-thin flame. The intense light produced by that flame was reflected about by the built-in reflector.

CC put the helmet on his head, and aimed it around the room. He was amazed by the illumination the light provided. Putting a handful of the calcium carbide in a pocket, he continued around the perimeter, stopping for a moment to peer into another tunnel that lay in the shadows of the far corner of the cave.

Continuing on around the cave, he came to a small plywood room, little bigger than a closet. When he opened the door, he was stunned. It had a concrete floor. On his left, there was a toilet; in the center, opposite the door, a lavatory; and on his right, a prefabricated shower stall. Everything was spotless. A towel hung neatly from a bar by the sink, and a plastic tray of cleaning supplies sat on the floor beneath it. A cabinet held an array of towels and first-aid supplies.

Closing the door, he came to another tunnel, the entry of which lay about three feet above the floor on which he was standing. A heap of empty food cans littered his approach to the ledge. It was a curious place for a refuse pile, and was inconsistent with the cleanliness of the bathroom.

He had to boost himself up waist-high to enter the passage, but before he could reach the ledge, an angry hen brushed past, scolding him as she flew down to the main floor. Her unexpected appearance had startled him, but this time, at least, he didn't panic.

The Nestling

The Cavern Behind the Barn
May 23rd, about 9:00 a.m.

Once again he started to climb up onto the ledge, but again there was a rustling sound, and something moved in the shadows. He leapt back to the cavern floor, almost tripping over his own feet, chary of any more encounters like the one he'd had with the snakes.

Then, as he stood in stunned silence, a little girl in soiled clothes emerged from the shadows. She blinked her eyes in the glare of his lantern, and with scarcely a quaver in her voice, she asked, "Did my grandpa send you to take grandma and me home?"

He just stood there, confusion warring with amazement. And while reason wrestled with emotion, she stood calmly on the ledge before him, her head tipped to one side, her hands on her hips, elbows extended outward. "What's the matter," she asked. "Cat got your tongue?"

Well, that was the beginning. Months later, CC would thank God for bringing this bright-eyed, big-hearted little girl into his life. She was to become a friend. Someone to talk with. Someone who needed him. Someone he needed. Yet now all he could think was, What will I do with her?

He tried to come to grips with the questions she had asked. It took a moment to get his thoughts in order before he replied.

"Well, in a way, I guess that your grandpa did send me here." He looked around, and asked, "Where is your grandma?"

In answer, she pointed her finger over her opposite shoulder into the darkness behind her. "Back there." She choked back a sob. "Grandma is very sick."

CC climbed onto the ledge, his acetylene headlamp dispelling little of the darkness, for the cave's ceiling rose high above their heads, and the tunnel widened at this point. He peered about, and in the shadows, a few yards back, he saw a form, covered with blankets, lying atop a cot. A smell, much like that in the house, nearly drove him back, but he steeled himself and made his way to the bed. He shined the light on the woman's face. Most of her hair had fallen out, her face was taut with pain, and bloody vomit stained her collar and blankets.

The light roused her, and she slowly turned her head toward him, raising a feeble hand to shield her reddened eyes against the glare. He quickly removed the appliance from his head, and aimed it at the nearby wall so that the reflected glow wouldn't dazzle her.

A feeble voice queried, "Who's there? Sarah, is that you?"

He replied, "No, ma'am. I happened by your farm, and I chanced to find you here."

"Who are you," she whispered. Her voice rasped, but it was determined. "Let me see your face."

"I'm sorry," he replied. "I don't know my name; I have amnesia."

She whispered something, and he knelt to hear her words. "The child, please, you must care for the child."

"Of course I will," he replied, absolute conviction in his voice. It had never occurred to him that he would do otherwise, though saying it made him wonder at his capacity to do so. "First thing, we'll get you cleaned up, and get some warm soup into you, and you'll be up and around in no time at all."

"No," she murmured, as though her situation was irrelevant. The merest smile turned her lips. "I'm going home." She looked up, trying to focus on him.

"You must do for her," she pleaded, and then gasped with pain, adding unnecessarily, "I don't have much time."

"Yes, ma'am, of course I will."

"Let me see your face," she demanded a second time, but her voice was so weak that he almost thought he'd imagined the words.

He held the lamp at arms length so that it flooded his face, and in so doing, blinded himself so that he could not see her reaction.

"You!" Her voice rose, and she tried to push herself up from the pillow. "Praise God, it's you." And she wept. Then she seemed to be talking to herself. "How could it be, Lord, that you could be so kind as to send this man to us?"

He had turned the light around and was inquiring quietly, but urgently. "Who?" he demanded. He almost wept, "Please," he pleaded, "who do you think I am?"

Her eyes were closing. "I'm coming, Joseph," she whispered, the tension gone from her voice. Then, with more energy, "I'm coming, Lord Jesus!" Then her body shuddered, and she lay still. Her hand, which had been tightly gripping his, relaxed and fell away. He still couldn't comprehend her excitement at seeing his face, as though he were someone special sent from God. She was probably hallucinating, he thought, but somehow he knew he was wrong. *How*, he wondered, *could she possibly recognize me?*

He knelt there for several minutes, numb with shock. Finally he came to himself, and began considering what he must do next. In the past fifteen minutes he'd discovered a cave full of farm animals, a little girl who needed a family, and a dying woman who seemed to know who he was. *First things, first*, he thought. *I need to take this little girl back to the farm house, clean her up, and feed her.*

"Grandma liked you," the child said thoughtfully, interrupting his deliberations. Unnoticed, she had moved up beside him. Then, taking charge, she reached out to take two of his fingers firmly in her hand, and turned to lead him toward the tunnel's entrance.

When he asked her what her name was, she responded proudly, "I'm Sarah Sennett, and I'm six years old."

He felt he had to speak with her about her family, but something more urgent — far more personal — was eating at him.

"Sarah," he asked. "Do you know who I am? I mean, have you ever seen me before?"

She looked at him carefully in the reflected light, pursed her lips in thought, and shook her head.

"Maybe a picture of me?" he pleaded.

Again she looked up at him as he knelt before her, holding the light toward his face as he had for her grandmother. She put her hands on her hips, bit her lip and stared at him. After a moment, she again shook her head from side to side. "Uh, uh," she answered. "I don't think so." And then, doubtfully, "Maybe on television?" Then, because she could see he was disappointed, she added, "I'm sorry."

And he, trying to hide his terrible disappointment, replied, "It's okay." Then he asked, "Sarah, why was your grandmother sick?"

"I don't know."

"Did she leave you alone and go outside the cave?"

"Oh, yes. She went to look for grandpa, and she didn't come back for a long time. After that is when she started being sick."

"Did your grandpa come back?"

"No. Grandma told her he was staying at the house."

"How long have you been in here?"

"I don't know. A long time. I almost ran out of cans of food."

"Well, you'll be alright now," he assured her, but he felt guilty making such an empty promise.

"I'd rather do it myself"

The Stable in the Cave

Hidden Valley

May 23rd, 5 p.m.

In spite of the loss of her family, Sarah appeared to rebound with the resilience of the very young. Her month in the cave with a dying woman notwithstanding, she had survived remarkably well. She told him that her grandma had taught her that she must keep herself clean, eat regular meals, and take a vitamin pill every day.

And, for the first week or so, her grandmother kept assuring her that God would send someone to care for her. CC wondered about how emotionally damaged the child might be until she offered the encouraging comment that she knew she would see her grandparents some day in heaven.

Before they'd left the cave, CC had questioned her closely enough to determine that her only memories were of her grandparents. She could offer no clue as to who or where her mommy and daddy were. He realized that, for the time being, he was all the family she had. He asked her how she came to be in the cave.

She spread her arms wide, spun in a circle, and said, "Grandpa made grandma and me hide in here. They told me that it was a game, like going camping." She frowned. "I knew it wasn't a game. Something was wrong, and after a while, I didn't like it. It's dark, and smelly. But I had to take care of grandma."

Concerned that the child might also be ill, CC repeated his earlier question, "How long were you here?"

"Grandpa said we had to stay here at least this many days." She held up both hands, fingers extended wide, then she squinted her eyes as she closed them to make fists, opening and closing them twice more.

Thirty days, CC thought. He wasn't taking any chances. No, that's not true. Obviously he took some sort of chance, and it cost him his life.

The little girl had gone on with her story. "Grandpa said there was something very bad outside, but that it would probably get tired of waiting, and go away."

Sarah showed him the light switch that illuminated the back of the cave where the old woman lay. It was obvious that the child's grandfather had prepared well for almost every eventuality. CC found empty canned good boxes and bottled water, an electric hot plate, stacks of children's books and toys, and a variety of other supplies and equipment that the old man had stored there. There was only one case of un-opened cans remaining, a popular brand of stew.

She was jabbering on, and pointed to the pile of opened cans. "I could open the ones with the little tabs on them, but I wasn't strong enough to use the can opener. That's why I'm glad you finally got here. I haven't had anything to eat since yesterday."

CC shuddered when he imagined the trauma the little girl must have endured during those lonely nights while her grandmother lay near death. Yet, on reflection, she'd fared very well when compared with the horror that millions of other children had experienced. At least she was alive and well.

Then it hit him. He'd been around the valley a couple of weeks, but she had run out of available food just the day be-fore. *This little girl was right. It was very close, and I showed up just in time. No wonder her grandmother seemed so happy. What an incredible coincidence.* He hung on that thought for a moment. *A coincidence?*

He wondered whether there might have been any way to stop this war — whether he might somehow have helped, and laughed at the possibility. Who was he, anyway? And then he realized it was pointless to ponder it. This hadn't been simply a break down in the financial system, or a collapse of the in-frastructure, or even the result of rampant immorality. They had contributed, but the entire world-wide catastrophe had been set up by billions of people filled with pride and selfish-ness who'd turned their backs on God.

And it was kick-started by unspeakable men who had yielded to the worst possible temptations. As far as CC was concerned, this was the result of men who thought themselves wise, but their foolish eyes were darkened, and they had simply become witting or unwitting servants of the devil. It was a matter of principalities and powers in the highest places yielding themselves up to oppose God. They'd sold their souls, and sacrificed the lives of billions to their own short-sighted greed, lust, and, ultimately, submission to Satan.

He realized with great sorrow that the war had probably been inevitable — that it is the nature of the race to hate and to fear and to kill. The only alternative was for people to embrace and share the love of Christ. Instead, they not only rejected Him, but attempted to stamp out the very message of His salvation.

CC recalled the prophecy: "In the last days, men will become lovers of selves...." And over the past several decades, it appeared obvious that most people had indeed become far more selfish. CC understood that this war was far worse than those that had gone before, that this was probably part of the grand and final cataclysm, the beginning of the end, the introduction to the great tribulation and the Apocalypse.

As he attempted to unravel these maudlin thoughts, the two of them left the cavern and walked back toward the Sennett house, the little girl skipping happily along, shading her eyes, no doubt delighted to once again see the familiar trees and grass of her home bathed in the glow of the midday sun. It was a strange contrast to the pervasive darkness of the cavern. When they reached the house, CC started to run a hot bath for her, then turned to help her with her clothing.

The child put her hands on her hips, elbows akimbo, and looked up at him in what he would come to realize was a characteristic pose.

"I can take my own bath, thank you."

She reached up as high as she could, put her hands on his belt buckle, and pushed him toward the bathroom door.

"If you want to do something for me, please get me a towel from the closet shelf. It's too high for me to reach."

When he returned, she instructed him to hang it on the door handle. Then she told him that he should go back to work.

"I'll have supper ready," she informed him, "when the little hand is on the five and the big hand is on the twelve."

He made them each a peanut butter sandwich and left hers on the table. Then he returned to the bathroom door to let her know that her lunch was ready.

"Thank you," she shouted above the noise of the shower, "but I'd rather do it myself."

And, an instant later, "Now you'd better take care of my grandma."

He could hear her voice break, and imagined that she had started to cry, but when he tried the handle, he found that she had locked the door. He knocked lightly, but she didn't reply. He didn't know whether to go or stay. How could he help a six-year old deal with her loss?

Before he could decide what to do, she asked if he was still there. When he replied that he was, she surprised him by saying quite offhandedly, "You need to clean the cave, too. The horses each drop about twenty-five pounds of manure every day."

He wondered whether her blithe statement might cover a reservoir of pain and confusion. If so, it would have to be dealt with before she would be whole again. And he suddenly realized that he could only help her by being available to her.

I must be as constant, steady and reliable as a rock. I'll need to instill a sense of confidence that there is some security and permanence in a very insecure and impermanent world.

Then he realized that he could not instill an idea that he did not embrace himself. Their future depended upon the grace of God.

That's right, he thought, a weight dropping from his shoulders. *The grace of God. I'll teach her what I know about God.*

I'll try to live what I know about God. And she can put her confidence in Him! We'll both put our confidence in Him.

Then he thought with irony, *Where else could we put our trust?* And another verse came to him. *"And the peace of God, which passeth all understanding, shall keep your hearts and minds through Christ Jesus."*

He spoke aloud. *"I would sure like to sense some of that peace today, Lord!"*

Later that day — with the physical and emotional trauma of a second burial weighing him down — he undertook the farm chores. Already tired, he spent a half hour using a shovel to push the manure in the cave into a compost pile. Then he replenished the feed, and milked the cow, though he wasn't sure he was very successful with that chore. The cow kicked the bucket over twice, spilling most of the milk. In spite of that, working with the animals had a strangely restorative effect on him.

When he returned to the house, dirty and tired, he was no longer depressed. Hard work seemed to have a salutary effect on him. And Sarah did indeed have a simple supper ready. Before he was permitted to eat, however, she insisted that he bathe, an exercise that he reluctantly undertook, but ultimately found enormously satisfying. And then they enjoyed their first meal together, canned spaghetti with meat balls, canned green beans, and fresh milk.

Nothing to write home about, if he'd had a home, but a wonderful meal in this day and time, and a very impressive demonstration by a small child.

The Hidden Valley Subway

Crossing the canyon underground
May 24th, about 10 a.m.

The next morning, CC left Sarah and headed back to continue his exploration of the caverns. He entered the underground barn and made his way to the ledge on which Sarah and her grandmother had sheltered.

As he reached the ledge, he noticed a heavy electrical cable that was fastened to the rock wall and ran back into the darkness. He followed the cable back through the subterranean barn and down the entry tunnel toward the farm buildings. It seemed clear to him that this was the means by which the electrical current flowed to the house. If the power flowed to the house, then its source had to lay in the opposite direction, directly through the tunnel in which he'd found the old woman.

CC got both the miner's lamp and a kerosene lantern going, and moved cautiously back along the passage. His former experiences beneath the surface left him a bit wiser. He'd anticipated the possibility of becoming lost, so he'd searched Sennett's barn and found a can of yellow spray paint. He planned to use it to spray arrows on the tunnel walls whenever he came to the intersection of another tunnel so that he could find his way back.

He passed through the area where he'd discovered Mrs. Sennett, and entered a natural tunnel. As he moved on, the tunnel floor and walls began to lean, and he soon found himself half walking, half crawling along the tilted surface. At one point he had to slide along on his back to avoid falling through a pot hole in the tunnel floor. Twisting so that he could look down through the hole, he could make out the surface of an underground stream perhaps six feet below.

He could not tell how deep the water was, nor how he'd get back up to this tunnel if the floor collapsed beneath him, so he began to take small mincing steps, careful to test the rock before trusting it to his entire weight. As he moved along this winding tunnel, he discovered several more pot holes that opened into other tunnels, not only in the floor, but in the side walls and ceiling as well.

The place was a virtual warren of pathways. The floor was rough, and seemed to rise as he went on. The light reflecting back from the walls and the ceiling changed from a soft doe color in some places to a mouse-gray in others. Using both the lamp on his helmet, and the lantern he carried in his hand, he moved carefully onward.

The cable periodically disappeared from view, buried in the silt beneath his feet. At one point, he leaned down to examine the printing that ran along its length. It was a very expensive heavy gauge copper, specially insulated for use underground and even underwater. He realized that a thick cable was required to maintain the voltage over what was obviously the long distance from the source of power to the farm house, and this one was carrying 220 volts.

It was waterproof because, just as obviously, parts of these tunnels flooded from time to time. The sediment that covered lengths of the cable offered mute testimony to that fact, and was a sobering reminder that he'd have to be careful about wandering these tunnels during rainstorms or during the winter melt when they might suddenly flood with water.

CC could hear a dull roaring from a gallery to his right, and he moved in that direction. Someone had worn a path in the dirt here, so he was less fearful of falling or becoming lost. Rounding a corner, he sprayed another of his yellow arrows on the rock wall. The sound of rushing water had become much louder, and he noted that the beam from his head lamp was not reflected back, but seemed to disappear into a great black void. He shouted, and his voice echoed back in the immensity of a vast low-ceilinged underground cavern.

This room was obviously much larger than any he had thus far discovered. He'd been taking short, mincing steps, making certain of his next move before lifting his weight from that foot. He stopped abruptly. A few feet from the edge of the shelf on which he was walking, his light was reflected across a broad smooth sheet of water. Its far edge was almost lost in the gloom, perhaps thirty or forty feet away. It appeared to be an underground lake, its black depths a mystery.

The rock walls seemed to soak up the light, and the golden corona that surrounded the lantern dazzled his eyes, at the same time leaving the deep reaches of the tunnel in velvety blackness. As he moved downstream, the sound of falling water had risen to a shattering crescendo in the rocky confines. Evidently, the lake ended in an underground waterfall.

He turned the lamp so that he could examine the cave wall beside him. He found no high water marks, no indication that the water ever rose above the banks that now contained it. He assumed that the high-water mark was beneath his feet, within the stream's natural channel. It was impossible to tell how far this little underground lake extended into the mountain's bowels, and he shivered when he thought of the possibility of trying to backtrack it.

A Subterranean Lake

North end of Hidden Valley
May 24th, late morning

CC lit a wooden match and flipped it into the water, then watched the flame sputter out as it was swept away to his right. As he followed the stone shelf downstream, the sound of falling water grew louder. He reached the end of the underground lake and was stunned to discover that the noise was caused by the stream pouring over a spillway on the far end of an underground dam. *More of old man Sennett's work?* he wondered, as he moved cautiously forward.

The concrete walkway atop the dam was about four feet wide, and perhaps thirty feet long, and he could see that it bridged the spillway near the far end. A railing made of rusty iron pipe ran the entire length on the downstream side of the walkway, but he nevertheless felt nervous about venturing out across the top of the massive structure.

CC took firm hold of the iron railing and tried to shake it. It moved slightly, but he thought that he could trust it. Leaning carefully out over the rusting barrier, he could see that the face of the dam below him sloped out toward the bottom, and was laid up of large, carefully dressed pieces of native stone. It was solidly built, its age indeterminable. Allowing for the darkness and any error in judgment, he estimated that it was perhaps fifteen feet to the water below, indicating that there would be a good head of pressure when the water reached the top of the dam, as it now did.

At the far end of the dam, the spillway was alive with foaming water, while the pool below was shrouded in spray and mist. Shining his gaslight to the left, he could see back over the lake above the dam, and estimated that it was at least fifty feet wide, narrowing to perhaps thirty feet at the point where the dam stood. Below the dam, there was a far smaller lake. It was only a guess, but he thought that the original waterway had probably cut a sharp groove down through the cave floor, and the builders were able to construct their dam at the narrowest point in the little subterranean canyon.

Several minutes passed while his eyes roved from place to place, taking in the details of this incredible installation. As he slowly crossed the top of the dam and started over the spillway, he felt the vibration from the water through his shoes. He finished walking gingerly across the spillway, gripping the railing with his right hand, carrying the gasoline lantern with his left.

A strange noise penetrated his consciousness, and he leaned out to identify its source. It suddenly occurred to him that he had discovered the source of the electricity. Beneath him, on the edge of the lower lake, revolved an old overshot wooden water wheel.

It was that steady creaking noise that he had been hearing, but had been unable to associate with the roar of the waterfall. The large wheel was powered by water from the spillway which ran through a pipe and dropped onto the buckets at the top of the waterwheel. The weight of the falling water carried the outside of the massive overshot wheel down and around, turning it on its thick central shaft, then spilling the spent water into a gutter on the slimy ledge below. From there it flowed into the pond below the dam.

He thought that it might have operated the milling equipment that had been used for crushing and pulverizing the limestone before it was heated to make cement. He reasoned that he must be somewhere near the cave entrance where the cement kilns stood. If so, that placed him just inside the mountain, immediately west of the fountainhead of the valley stream, and perhaps two hundred yards south of the entrance to his cave.

He looked down on his immediate right and noticed a stone stairway that led down to the platform. The stairway was parallel to the water wheel on his right, with a pipe handrail. He carefully made his way down the slippery treads, holding carefully to the old railing and watching to see that the steps had not broken away below his feet.

The falling water filled the entire cave below the dam with fog, and the lantern's glow gave the place a cold, hellish appearance. The milling machinery on the ledge was scabrous with rust. As he drew closer, he saw that it was frozen with corrosion, an immovable mass of rusty junk. CC ripped a rotting sheet of canvas as he attempted to pull it off an old-fashioned corn sheller. The machine was still connected to the shaft of the water wheel by a broad leather belt. Several bushels of rotting corn lay in a heap on the ground next to the machine.

CC pulled his eyes away from the equipment to focus on the wheel that towered above his head. Drops of water splashed upon him, and the noise of the wheel creaking through its revolutions was much louder here. Some of the wooden braces had recently been replaced, and the wheel itself looked to be in excellent condition. Originally, the main shaft probably ran through wooden journals that would have been liberally lubricated with a heavy grease. This shaft, however, was steel, and the wheel that turned round it was mounted on sealed ball bearings.

The wheel moved ponderously, slowly turning on its massive shaft. This in turn rotated a series of cog wheels which ultimately spun a shaft at a very high speed, powering the generator.

It's incongruous, he thought, *an eighteenth century wooden water wheel turning the shaft of a twenty-first century portable electrical generator.*

He was mesmerized by what seemed nothing short of a miracle. Here he was, in a world that had used its sources of power to destroy all of its sources of power, and he, a hopeless refugee, had discovered what was probably one of the few remaining sources of hydroelectric power in America.

This, then, explained the refrigeration and lighting in the Sennett's farm house. He laughed aloud.

So, America had four grids, he thought. *The Eastern, the Western, the Texans', and "The Sennett Grid."*

It was a fantastic find, and he felt strangely compelled to drop to his knees for a moment and offer thanks to the One who was obviously guiding his steps.

He thought of the Sennett's cozy little cottage with regret. He'd already decided that he didn't dare occupy their lovely house for it seemed certain to be discovered.

So now, if at all possible, he hoped to redirect this electrical cable to his cavern and somehow make it serve his needs. Sennett had obviously generated sufficient power from the water wheel to satisfy his limited electrical needs, so if he could find a way to reroute it to his cave, he would be able to enjoy many conveniences including the operation of an occasional appliance or power tool.

There is, he thought, *a huge difference between washing clothes by standing in an icy stream and pounding them with a rock as opposed to throwing them into a clothes washer and returning at the end of the cycle when a bell rings.* And the possibility of operating a water

heater, refrigerator, dishwasher, electric stove, or even a microwave oven, suggested unimaginable luxury.

He looked again at the little generator, and realized that
it was too small to handle most of those chores. But it would
handle some of them. Yes, he smiled, it would handle some.
Unfortunately, he had no idea where his cavern was in rela-
tion to this dam, nor how he could reroute the heavy cable.

His mind was a ferment of ideas. If the machinery he
was looking at was in reasonably good condition, it would require only routine maintenance. And hidden beneath the
earth as it was, the water wheel would never freeze in winter.
He would remove the cable that was supplying the farm
house, so that no chance visitor could trace it through the caverns as he had. He could use the same waterproof cable to
route the power to his new underground home. And no one
would ever have cause to suspect the existence of this little
power station.

If he weren't seeing it with his own eyes, he would never
have believed it. His mind raced. We wouldn't have to burn
wood to warm ourselves. I wouldn't have to cut down trees,
split the logs, transport the heavy wood, store it in damp
caves, maintain dangerous fires, and find a way to get rid of
the ash and creosote. There would be no need to leave scars
on the landscape by cutting trees for firewood, scars that
would be noticed by unwelcome visitors.

In addition, he would avoid the additional danger that
the smoke from a fire would reveal their presence. And hydroelectric heat would be green. It would do away with all the
heavy, time-consuming and dangerous labor of burning
wood, and it would leave virtually no imprint.

Lighting the cavern would have presented another prob-
lem. Nineteenth-century man had been able to advance from
the use of candles and oil lamps to gas lights. Yet, it has been
little more than a century since the brighter, safer electric
lamp had been introduced. And recently there'd been a

switch to high-efficiency lamps, such as fluorescents and LEDs.

When he'd loaded those super-efficient light fixtures and lamps at the home improvement warehouse, he'd questioned the wisdom of his decision, for his small stock of gasoline and kerosene would not run his portable generator for very long. He did have a couple of solar panels, but mounting them outside the cave would require that he run the cable up the tunnels, and they would be visible to any unwanted visitors.

And with an inexhaustible source of electricity, he would also avoid going through the difficult business of gathering materials to try to make primitive lamps, or the time-consuming job of making smelly and dangerous candles. He was ecstatic until he began to consider the amount of work that would be involved.

A source of electricity would ease many of the everyday burdens of living. To a person who must be virtually self-sufficient, these are the issues of life. It would provide the means to keep clothing, cooking utensils, and bodies cleaner, healthier, and more comfortable. A hot bath had become an indescribable luxury which he had formerly taken for granted, as had a supply of artificial light to read by. If he could harness this power, he would not be a person lost in the shadows. Then his thoughts turned maudlin. *We are all lost in the shadows — a world facing its second dark age.*

A steering wheel from a big truck was mounted horizontally on a shaft that rose out of the floor about waist high. He turned the wheel a little, and the volume of water moving over the top of the water wheel increased. It splashed onto the wooden paddles, and then, with what sounded like a scream of resentment or joy, the old wheel began to revolve faster. He pulled a lever, and power was transmitted to another shaft, and he could hear the sound of a machine across the platform grinding whatever residue remained within its maw. He quickly disengaged the lever and returned the steering wheel to its original position. The speed of the water-wheel slowed.

Turning his head so that the lamp illuminated the generator, he could see that it continued to operate smoothly. There was a switch box fastened to a panel on the wall behind the generator. He assumed it would enable him to shut down the electrical power at any time.

A feeling of exultation swept over him as he stood and watched the big wheel make its slow and immensely powerful sweeps, the weight of the falling water developing the sort of enormous horsepower which nineteenth-century Americans harnessed so cheaply to power their industrial revolution.

As the wheel began to turn faster, he became concerned about generating too high a voltage, or too many amperes, but his benefactor had provided for that possibility. Near the circuit switch box was an ammeter and a device for controlling voltage levels. And there was a light switch. After looking at the neoprene-coated cables, CC concluded that this electrical generator had been added many years after the water wheel.

CC checked to see whether he was standing in a puddle. Then — wondering what might be the result — he flicked the switch. The area was instantly flooded with light. At least it seemed so to someone who'd been walking in near darkness for hours. There were a half-dozen bulbs mounted in waterproof glass shades above the dam and around the platform on which he was standing. A yellow haze surrounded each bulb where spray and fog caught the light. CC began to laugh uncontrollably as they illuminated the dam.

He peered across the platform toward the far end of this little lake at the bottom of the dam. He could tell by the darker shadows that the cavern narrowed about fifty feet downstream from the water wheel, and that the roof of the cave also dropped down toward the surface of the water. He was looking for the tunnel through which the overflow from the dam must pass.

He thought he could detect a whirlpool near the far side of the pond, an indication that the water was disappearing through a submerged tunnel. Surely this had to be the source of the stream that ran down the center of the valley.

He thought he might be seeing the top edge of a submerged tunnel on the far side of the little lake. *What would happen,* he wondered, *if the amount of water passing over the dam was so great that it overflowed the drainage tunnel? Would it flood this area in which he was standing, leaving the generator and waterwheel underwater?*

He examined the end of the cavern above the lake. He noticed what looked like a second tunnel through the face of the sheer rock wall just above the water line. It had obviously been carved to carry off excess flood water. Both tunnels were just beyond the whirlpool, but there was no way in the world he could get to the far side of the pool to examine them.

Picking up a piece of scrap wood, he flipped it out into the water. Nearly waterlogged, it was swiftly drawn across the surface and sucked into the whirlpool, quickly disappearing from sight. There should have been some illumination where the stream exited the mountain, but there was no sign of daylight. It supported his earlier conclusion that the stream exited through a submerged cave or tunnel, and flowed back to the surface as a spring — probably the pool he'd seen at the base of the cliff.

If he dared leave Sarah alone out in the valley, where the stream down the valley originated beneath the cliffs, perhaps he could pour a box of clothing dye into the water here, and she would be able to tell him if it colored the water where she was waiting. If that were the case, he knew that there was little likelihood of anyone ever discovering this underground dam.

He checked the technical data on the generator name plate. It had only 6,500 watts capacity, but it was 100% duty-cycle, and that explained why Sennett could leave it running day after day. CC realized that the capacity was far too small to power more than one or two appliances at a time. It simply couldn't stand up to heavy service. If, however, he could get hold of a generator large enough to produce sufficient electricity to heat an underground house, his options would be nearly unlimited. His mind churned with the possibilities.

He returned his attention to the machinery with something akin to awe. He wondered at the skill, courage, and energy that it took to build this dam, especially when he realized how just the din of the roaring water, and the vibration that seemed to shake the earth, was dulling his own senses. He couldn't imagine anyone building a cofferdam here, let alone erecting a dam and setting up this impressive subterranean water wheel.

Gone, at least for the moment, was his fear of the future. This was incredible. A miracle of Providence. He was rich in things that really mattered, but he didn't feel that way. He instead felt like a poor man who had found a buried treasure, and, since he no longer needed to spend his time worrying about starving, he instead devoted himself to worrying about losing his new-found wealth.

He found the noise and flickering lights to be enervating, slowly eroding his confidence and strength. A vague sense of insecurity, even fear, began to gnaw at him. The reflecting lights and the constant din were beginning to work on his mind. He had a strange feeling, standing below that dam. He watched the condensation drip down the slimy rocks, saw where water trickled through the joint between two loose stones, and imagined that the entire dam wall was bulging under the enormous pressure of the lake that was trapped behind it, and was about to crush him as it swept him away.

It occurred to him that it probably wouldn't take much in the way of explosives to level this dam and empty the lake. *Now why would I consider such a thing,* he wondered. He realized that he had no sense of night or day, and was suddenly caught by the phenomenon that grips many people after they have been beneath the earth's surface for awhile. His watch told him it was still early afternoon, but he felt as though it was the middle of the night.

He suddenly felt that he had to get out of there and he found himself almost incapacitated with fear. The stairway was very slippery, and he found himself crawling up the stairs on all fours lifting the lantern step by step and gripping the railing with his left hand. When he reached the top, he forced himself to his feet, holding firmly to the railing, and carefully made his way back across the dam.

Although this bout with claustrophobia was less debilitating than an earlier attack, an almost overwhelming desire grew in him to run from this place, to escape to the outdoors where he'd find sunlight and trees.

The Farmer in the Dell

The Sennett Farm
May 24th to 29th

During the days that followed he didn't give much thought to what he'd come to laughingly call his "hydroelectric project." He actually came to the point where he derided the idea because it seemed increasingly ridiculous.

Just the idea of uprooting the existing heavy cable, which had to be nearly a thousand feet long, would be a daunting if not impossible task. Add to that the unlikelihood of discovering a tunnel that might connect the cavern containing the dam to the one in which he'd parked his motor home, and the entire project seemed impossible.

So it merely hovered on the periphery of his thoughts. He hadn't even moved back from the Sennett house to the motor home, in spite of his earlier determination to do so. There was simply too much else to occupy him.

His immediate concern had been for Sarah and the farm. The animals were both a blessing and a curse. A blessing, of course, because of the meat, eggs, milk, butter, and cheese that could be produced. The horses were invaluable because of their ability to help plant and harvest crops and move heavy loads. Even their manure was valuable as fertilizer. They were a curse, because he had to care for the milk producers twice daily, and the ages-old enslavement of the farmer to his stock was manifesting itself.

It was not simply the hard work. It was living by a schedule, and that schedule was dictated by the demands of the animals and the seasons of the year. And though Sarah proved herself a wonderful help by caring for the poultry and preparing an occasional light meal, the heavy burdens rested with him. Beyond that, he realized that he must soon take time from other projects in order to try to provide for her education.

It seemed to him that he would either have to relocate somewhere near the farm, or situate the animals closer to his cave. He remembered that several partially overgrown fields lay fallow between the wood road and the cliffs near his cave. Perhaps he could pasture them there. On the other hand, if he moved them, they might attract attention. He would need to shelter them in bad weather and find a place to milk the cow.

Regardless of where I keep the animals, I will still have to mow hay and store it somewhere. So why don't I simply replicate Sennett's underground barn on my side of the valley? I certainly have plenty of room in the caverns. I really don't want to let the livestock run loose to be at the mercy of predators and disease. And it would help keep them safe from both radiation and predators.

As far as the poultry was concerned, he could leave enough food in Sennett's hen coop for several days, but if he didn't pick up the eggs, they would spoil or the flock would grow. And a growing flock would require more food. And hens needed light to lay. So to keep the size of the flock down, he decided to keep the two roosters in separate cages for the time being. *That ought to make them crow,* he thought.

Above all, he was nagged by the growing realization that he needed more help, and the prospect of finding anyone suitable seemed extremely remote. There was no question that he would not be able to travel back and forth across the valley morning and evening to milk the cow, let alone during a January blizzard, but he didn't see any reason why he couldn't build some stalls and a chicken coop in the mouth of one of his caves, an expedient that would allow him to move most of the animals nearer.

The morning after he buried Sarah's grandmother, he had taken a half hour to sweep a scintillator back and forth over the vegetable garden and had found no measurable radioactivity. At first he planned to play it safe. Because he had adequate stores of food for at least a couple of years, he thought to harvest the early crop — lettuce, radishes, broccoli, beans, and carrots — then discard it in the corner of the valley. That would, he concluded, be better than risking any possibility of radiation poisoning entering their food chain.

Since he found no indication of radiation, however, and the fresh produce would be a meaningful addition to their diets, he decided to harvest the little they could use in their daily meals. He planned to use a sensitive detector to check the produce as he washed each batch for use. Later in the summer, if they were able to harvest such things as tomatoes, squash, pumpkins, and potatoes, they would store or can whatever they could.

Things would be different next year, he decided. They wouldn't be planting in Sennett's garden plot. In a way, that was too bad. Those folks had done a wonderful job of composting, and the loam was very rich and dark. In fact, the actual garden plots were raised about a foot above the surrounding land. He hoped he could compensate for the loss of this high-quality soil by following the directions he'd found in a book on hydroponic gardening, and hoped to establish a vegetable garden in the sunlit mouth of one of the caves on his side of the valley.

That's how he'd come to think of the valley now, with everything north of the stream as "his side of the valley," and everything on the south side as the Sennett Farm, and off limits.

He decided that he'd also probably plant some small and irregular patches of corn and wheat in the meadows on his side of the valley. It would be more troublesome to cultivate irregular patches, but also more difficult for a pilot to identify them from the air. He was concerned that sooner or later someone would come looking for the Sennetts, and he wanted to limit the possibility of their stumbling onto him by accident.

That night that he found Sarah in the cavern, he laid a fire on the hearth in the Sennett house. As he sat in a recliner before the fire assessing his day, she lay curled up on the sofa, listening to music, the dog asleep at her feet. CC was still musing over the meal she'd prepared. After dinner, she also insisted that she would wash the dishes, but she did permit him to help by drying them and putting them on the cupboard shelves because they were difficult for her to reach. She stood on a special stool her grandpa had made to enable her to reach the sink. Now she lay on the sofa in a thrall, the fourth movement of the "Symphony from the New World" thundering through the house.

His thoughts returned to more serious business. He had gone through the entire house with his scintillator and found no significant levels of radiation. He had no desire to go back into the Sennett's bedroom, and had closed the door against an almost palpable spiritual darkness. He shivered in spite of the warm fire. He'd used a vacuum cleaner over the entire house, then discarded the disposable bag by carrying it off with a shovel. The house seemed clean, but he would not want to live here. And tonight he would sleep in the reclining chair, if he slept at all.

He began to leaf through the books that had been left laying about, decided they were of little interest at the moment, and stacked them to the side. Then he began searching through the desk to learn more about the Sennetts, and perhaps get a hint of more secrets of their valley. At first he felt he was intruding, but then he realized he had a need to understand them because he was now assuming the role of guardian to their granddaughter.

He regretted that Sarah's grandparents were not alive, not simply because of any burden that Sarah might represent to him, nor because they might have been allies, but because he realized that they would have been fascinating acquaintances, even good friends.

He was still troubled by the dying woman's joyous insistence that she knew him. He couldn't help but hope that something in the house, a photograph, diary, or old newspaper, might help solve the riddle of why they had lived in this remote place, and maybe even help him discover his own identity. Apart from that, the name "Sennett" seemed to somehow awaken memories, and even a sense of foreboding. He shook the growing depression away. He couldn't afford to readjust his mindset on the basis of emotions. One thing he knew, their knowledge of an outsider like himself seemed inconsistent with their reclusive life style.

"I wonder," he thought aloud, "whether there is a Sennett in my past." Sarah's eyes opened slightly at the sound of his voice, so he lifted her in his arms and carried her off to her bed. It had been her bedroom door which had remained closed when he'd first entered the house, and he was happy to learn that it held no more unhappy secrets for him.

It was a wonderful feeling, holding another living human being, and he realized at that moment that she actually gave him a reason for living. Perhaps, he thought, I have children of my own somewhere. If so, hopefully someone else is caring for them as I'm trying to care for Sarah.

He slumped back into the old overstuffed recliner, but did not give himself over to tears. For some reason they seemed terribly appropriate and he felt the need to weep over so many things, but when he tried to isolate a single cause, none seemed quite sufficient. He had seen much death, and one or two additional bodies should make little difference. What's more, Sarah somehow represented a compensation for the horrors he'd seen, proof that while there will always be the dead and the dying, life does go on.

"It's just the fact of being involved, of being so near to the victims that I identify with them," he thought aloud.

CC rose and walked to the windows, pulling the curtains tight against the dangers, real or imagined, hidden in the darkness outside. Then he allowed this fragile, man-made environment to reshape his mood.

The cheerful fire snapping on the hearth, its dancing light in counterpoint to the rosy aura of the ruby-shaded oil lamps, the rich hearty smell of the steaming coffee by his chair, and the swelling grandeur of Dvorak's great music, all served to lift the gloom from the little house, and carry him back to happier times. For a few moments, at least, he could pretend to live in a world that no longer existed, and lose himself in the light, the sound, and the warmth of this remote cottage.

It offers an illusion of durability and timeliness, he thought, *or is it merely an illusion? Am I not enjoying as great comfort as I've ever known? Is my perspective warped by my knowledge of the suffering and pain I've witnessed?* He gazed around him. *This marvelous collection of books must have seemed real and honest to their writers, and were obviously treasured by the Sennetts. They might also trigger my own imagination, and take me back through time and space to help me shut out the rude temporal realities for a few moments.*

He started to select some of the fine old classics, but then found himself stacking whole sets on chairs and tables. Dare he take these, and the bookcases themselves, to his less comfortable but much safer cavern?

CC found himself in the easy chair again, leafing through the books. He knew that sleep would elude him in spite of the fact that he was seriously concerned about adequate rest. He must, he knew, be careful to maintain a regular schedule in order to protect his mind and body. For while he delighted in the liberty to do as he desired, he also recognized the freedom as a dangerous illusion, for no man who must take responsibility for himself and others is ever truly free.

Freedom exacts a great price, he thought. *It requires individual responsibility, as well as the risks and labors associated with that respon - sibility. That's something that most Americans had either forgotten or had never learned, probably the latter, and because of that they have paid a huge price. They relinquished the authority for their own lives and liber - ties in exchange for the empty promises that a faceless government could and would make better decisions than they could make for themselves.*

Worse, they trusted the venial, power-hungry politicians to provide them with security, not realizing that every dollar they sent to Washington had an incredible percentage removed to cover bureaucratic overhead, plain outright thievery, and "reallocation" of assets. Finally they'd found them - selves drawn into treachery that resulted in privation, war, and the death of a nation.

Character is the cornerstone of good government, he thought. *When we elected someone on the basis of his promises, we needed to be able to count on his sticking to the principles that undergirded those prom - ises. Unfortunately, we had largely become a nation of opportunistic liars and cheats, and once the electorate became disillusioned, chaos was in - evitable. Well, it's over,* he thought. *I suppose we've gotten what we de - serve. Now, for a while, it's every man for himself.*

CC tucked his head into the corner of the chair, closed his eyes, and with the firm certainty of sleeplessness that was born of excitement and fatigue, his body fooled him. A book slipped from his slack hands, and he slept.

Hours later he drew his knees up, seeking unconsciously to remain warm. The fire had died, and the chill of the mountain dawn permeated the house. He pulled himself stiffly out of the chair and made his way to the hearth where he stirred the coals and added a couple of logs. Then he put on another pot of the precious coffee, and sat back to con - sider yesterday's great discoveries. Staring abstractedly at the dog asleep on the hearth, he thought of the adorable little girl, and his burden to provide for her.

Perhaps that was the reason that he couldn't dispel the vision of the great water wheel turning slowly in the murk of the cavern. He shook his head as though to clear away the impossibility of his fantasy. Try as hard as he could, he was unable to rid himself of his preoccupation with that cavern. If he could somehow generate enough electricity, he'd have a labor-free source of clean heat with no residue or smoke.

And even if anyone did fly over the valley with infra-red detection equipment, they would be unlikely to spot his shelter. The huge mass of rock in the mountain above his cave would easily absorb and dissipate the relatively small amount of heat, as well as any infra-red signature he might generate.

So the question haunted him. How could he generate enough electricity to power his appliances, then direct the current to his cave? The water wheel would certainly produce all the energy he needed, but how could he convert that to electricity? He needed something bigger than the small generator that it now powered.

It was as he slept that he was somehow reminded of the standby generator at the hospital in Deep River Junction. That machine had kept the lights in the hospital's basement burning for nearly two weeks, and when he had shut it down, it still had not exhausted the fuel in the storage tank.

CC wasn't interested in the diesel engine which powered the hospital generator. He wanted the generator itself. His thought was to somehow dismount it, get it back here, and attach it to the water wheel. It would provide all of the power he would ever need. But getting such a heavy machine into the cavern, down over the edge of the dam to the deck below, and mounted to the water wheel — those tasks would present enormous challenges. He knew that he'd have to deal with them one at a time, but before he could consider undertaking that project, he needed to get the farm in order.

He set some priorities. He had to provide for the long-term care of the livestock, plant more vegetables, begin construction of his permanent cave home, and prepare for winter. And, of course, he needed to provide continual care for Sarah.

He sat at Joseph's desk for over an hour, making lists, searching through books, taking notes, figuring out what to do and how to do it. Once in a while, he'd discover an old photo or some letters, and find himself wasting precious minutes trying to unravel the mystery of this hidden valley.

He was reluctant to reenter the Sennett bedroom, but he finally returned there to lay a note on the bed that provided the date he'd buried the old man and explaining that he had buried his wife beside him. He had signed the note, "CC."

It was as he was leaning over to drop the note on the box spring that he stubbed his toe on something beneath the edge of the bed. Kneeling, he found a large diary, with the year embossed on its hard cover in gold leaf.

Sennett's Diary

Sennett Cottage

Hidden Valley

May 26th, 8:30 p.m.

CC carried the diary back to the great room, flopped down in the easy chair, and turned to the first page. It was a thick book, beautifully bound in black leather, with "Joseph Sennett, Sr." embossed in gold on the cover.

He spent several hours over the next two nights leafing through the book. Sennett had been a Christian author and speaker, but when he began to impact the political picture across America, his reputation had been systematically destroyed. His entries were, to say the least, colorful.

"Three years ago today, we moved here to our 'stronghold' because we were forced to abandon our call to reach a world with the practical message of the love of Christ. In countering our message, our enemies found a more effective means of disposing of us than crucifixion.

"Our detractors are masters of the politics of personal destruction, and they systematically destroyed our reputations as well as our ministries. The media first painted us with the excrement of lies, as others once did to Jesus. Then, in a conspiracy of silence, the media — dominated by immoral and amoral writers and commentators — submerged us in the offal of anonymity. Martyrdom would have been better. Then, at least, our innocent blood might have cried out from beyond the grave."

CC moved on quickly, scanning a page here, a paragraph there. Somehow he knew that the account was true, but his review of the information was immediately accompanied by a severe headache, and he was forced to stop reading. Nevertheless, he was intrigued with Sennett's explanation of how his life was undermined, and in spite of his headache, found himself continually returning to his account.

"Our ministry had been reaching millions, and our reputation was as clean as the driven snow. We lived simple, godly lives, and gave all of our income to the ministry, receiving back only a modest annual salary barely sufficient for our needs. We did not own fancy houses or automobiles, eat at expensive restaurants, buy costly jewelry, or travel for pleasure. We had our financial records audited annually by a big four accounting firm. The real estate we owned had been in our family from before the Revolution, and we struggled simply to pay the taxes on two large tracts of worthless land.

"I suppose we were naive, but when the attacks began, we were surprised and hurt. They began with half-truths. Then, clearly a conspiracy, the sensationalist tabloids all began front-page smear campaigns against us. Even the way they phrased their headlines was almost identical. Within hours, the network news people picked up on it, asking, *Gee whiz, can this be true?* Then they reasoned, *Why not? Other religious leaders have done things like this.*"

"In spite of the fact that the world is overrun by war, pestilence, and distress of nations, it seemed that my wife and I had become the subject of interest for the lead story on the evening news and for the front page of every daily paper. The spin doctors flooded the Web with half-truths and innuendo."

CC was inexplicably upset, and needed an excuse to interrupt his reading, so he went to the kitchen to refill his coffee cup. Then he resumed his reading.

"But I was not without friends. And after millions of letters of outrage flooded their offices, and subscriptions were canceled and advertising revenue dropped, they grudgingly admitted that there might just be a small backlash. They finally concluded that even if everything they reported wasn't true, they were justified in taking frequent close looks at conservative Christians, because, they argued, *Where there's smoke, there's fire.*"

"They were the ones blowing smoke," Sennett quipped, "and they are the ones who will inevitably feel the fire." He continued, "In spite of my clear understanding of what was going on, I couldn't relate to or accept their descriptions of my wife and myself. They didn't resemble us in any way. And, for two people who had always sought to avoid even the appearance of evil, it was devastating. We began losing friends and supporters. The worst shock came from other people in the ministry who had always acted as our friends."

Now Sennett began to deal with his disillusionment.

"My wife couldn't accept this duplicity. How could those who had espoused love for us be so treacherous? Was it the result of some secret jealousy by others at our success in reaching the lost? Was it ambition to displace us? Did they not realize that by attacking God's people, they were aiding the enemy in his attack against the entire Body of Christ? The greatest irony was that many of the attacks came from within the Church, even from reporters at respected Christian journals.

"They would actually put us on camera, ask us thus and so, and then, when they edited the videotape, would use our reaction to one question as our response to a totally unrelated subject, thus totally twisting our views in the viewer's mind. This frequent practice successfully confused their listeners and made us look bad.

"Then came the silence! The attacks stopped abruptly. The news commentators ceased to even mention our names. Our photos no longer graced the covers of the scandal sheets. If supporters wrote letters to the editors, they were not printed. It was part two of their conspiracy, a conspiracy of silence. During the smear campaign, they perverted every press release that we produced, and used every interview we granted to spin and manipulate our statements.

"When their campaign of destruction began, we monitored dozens of radio and TV personalities who all used the same key phrases to attack us. It was clearly a conspiracy, patently dishonest but incredibly effective, for the various media worked in harmony, first publicizing false charges, then suddenly and completely ignoring us.

"Figuratively speaking, we were accused, judged, executed, buried, and forgotten, all in a period of two weeks. It became clear that the press and the media manipulated the mind of America, bringing anything they wished to the forefront of public attention, then sweeping it aside to promote or attack something else.

"What the world never learned was that the IRS reversed our ministry's long-standing tax exemption. The income from offerings dried up, and we soon ran out of money. Our TV and radio programs were canceled, even by Christian stations.

"Then our books mysteriously disappeared from the shelves in the bookstores and the public libraries. We were left with no means of reaching the public. Our only means of reaching even our most loyal supporters was through costly mass mailings or via the Internet. Somehow even the mass mailings were lost or misdirected, and our web site was repeatedly shut down by hackers. Income dried up. It was as if we had never existed."

CC set the diary down, and walked to the fireplace where he stared unseeing at the glowing logs. Returning to his chair, he thought, *This is intense stuff.* He felt that he was familiar with this story, though his mind seemed to refuse to deal with it, to blank it out. He actually got a severe headache while reading it. He nonetheless believed that what Sennett had written was true.

He stopped to ponder this man who had made a tremendous impact on the nation, for he had a nagging memory of Joseph Sennett. It seemed strange, for he was still unable to remember his own background, but he somehow remembered both the love and the hatred that had been heaped on this venerable preacher. He remembered the man's noble compassion for those with whom he disagreed, as well as his honesty in approaching any issue. And he remembered when Sennett had slipped from the public eye.

It was right after we were on the radio together, he remembered.

He sat bolt upright, his face twisted in shock.

I was on a radio program with Joseph Sennett?

As soon as the thought appeared, it fled from him, as though he was forced to relinquish it for the sake of sanity. It was as though the gasses in a log on the hearth had exploded, and a spark had landed on his clothing, forcing him to brush it away before he was burned. He simply could not bring himself to follow this line of thought.

Yet he felt compelled to return to the diary. Even though it only spoke of a life that had been, Sennett's words burned like fire. To CC, the words were alive and relevant, and could not be altered by any perverted recidivism. The cries of pain and confusion which Sennett had penned, perhaps to retain his own sanity, rang with both truth and despair for the state of a fallen church and nation.

Sennett had attained a certain noble immortality through his words. He was far more alive than those who had sought to destroy him. Though the words seemed to convey the thoughts of a man whose dreams were broken and forgotten, it was not so. For if anyone were to read his words with care, they would be impressed with his unfailing courage, and inevitably they would realize that Sennett had not been broken by his circumstances.

CC riffled casually through the diary, reading wherever the pages fell open. The man was certainly a profound writer. And he was clearly a good planner and a hard worker. This was evidenced in how he had lived. And it was obvious that the minister and his wife had been as skilled with other tools as with pen and ink.

The farm was beautifully built and maintained, the house was well-stocked with food, clothing, books, and medical supplies. Numerous items of fine homemade clothing and furniture attested to this. And if they'd been able to escape to the cavern as he'd obviously planned, they would have survived, while most of their detractors had died largely as a result of their own sins.

Both Sennett and his wife had obviously been voracious readers, for there were two desks, each reflecting their respective tastes and interests. Upon hers, neatly placed in the precise center, CC found a Bible open to the book of Job. Just to its right lay a book of poetry; it was opened to Eliot's, "The Love Song of J. Alfred Prufrock."

Her husband's desk was not as neat, with a stack of books and a farmer's almanac in one corner, and another Bible. His was opened to "Peter," with the passage about the earth being dissolved with a fervent heat circled in red ink. CC's mind turned back to the cataclysmic exchange of nuclear weapons which might have dissolved this earth had not some strange and unknown circumstance arisen to halt the destruction.

He set the diary aside for later reading and began to browse through their music collection. He selected one of Wagner's works, the "Prelude to Die Meistersinger," and turned the volume down so as not to disturb the child. As the piping of the brass gave way to the sweeping strings, he again marveled at the source of the electricity that powered the sound system. It was an anachronism in a world gone mad, and he was suddenly determined to capitalize on this precious asset.

He looked through the open bedroom door where Sarah was curled up asleep on her own bed, and his lips turned up in a smile.

At her feet was her large pink backpack. That afternoon, she'd taken great pains to stuff it with her clothing and favorite belongings in anticipation of their trip back to his cave in the morning. She was very excited about staying in the motor home and had made him provide a detailed description of her new home.

Sennett's Last Words

Sennett Cottage
Hidden Valley
May 28th, 10:20 p.m.

Two nights later, CC resumed reading Sennett's diary. The evening had been unseasonably warm, and he didn't bother lighting a fire.

Sarah had fallen asleep so he turned to the final entries in the chronicles of a man's life, entries made just three weeks before. There was no entry for April 22nd. That was the morning that CC remembered awakening in the Deep River Junction hospital, the day the war had begun.

"April 23rd, 3 a.m. No time to write yesterday; newscaster said there was an exchange of nuclear weapons. It's unclear as to which nations are involved, except we were obviously on the receiving end. It began about noon. With no radio in the old truck, I might not have known, but I was making a rare visit to my old friend's feed store, and he and his wife were listening to reports on the radio when I arrived.

"All of our aircraft carriers were conveniently moored side-by-side in Newport News and San Diego, a violation of common sense, if not long-standing Navy policy since the loss of our fleet of battleships at Pearl Harbor in 1941. It made for easy destruction by our enemies, and with most of our nuclear missiles destroyed by our last two presidents, it's unlikely that we could have retaliated, even if there'd been the desire.

"While the three of us stood on the front porch of the feed store, we could actually see flashes in the sky, as bright as the sun, hundreds of miles to the south and east. We even heard faint rumbles. Nothing nearby; I don't think that they hit Albany or Burlington, but almost certainly Boston and New York.

"When I finally returned home, Sandra and Sarah were not in the house. They'd obviously followed my instructions and sheltered in the cave with the livestock. I had set up three cots in the cave because we wanted to be prepared for any eventuality. We live far from any possible assistance, and if the house ever burned down, I seriously doubt that anyone would ever know about it, let alone come to our aid.

"I've always figured the cave would be a good place to go in the event of an emergency, especially during the winter. For years, I've kept extra food, clothing, medicine, and bedding there in case of a crisis. With a year-round temperature of 52 degrees, it makes a wonderful warehouse and fruit cellar. And it's been great for the animals in the winter because the cave is warmer than the barn.

"Sometimes Sandy and I would go up there, and we'd talk or read. Sarah loved to play there. It was a one-girl petting zoo, and she could let her imagination create all sorts of marvelous fantasies. It was Sarah's responsibility to feed the chickens, geese, and ducks. And she loved to pet the sheep, especially the lambs. I built a simple bathroom, and even had electric lights by which we could work and read.

"If all had gone as planned, I'd have returned to the farm before the fallout started coming down, but I'd loaded five-hundred pounds of feed in the back of the old pickup, and a tire blew, and it took me a couple of hours to walk the rest of the way home. So for all my preparations for emergencies, my oversight would prove fatal. When I got to the house, I felt a bit off, and immediately started writing this."

The next entry was at 5 p.m.

"I was feeling nauseous and I had to lay down on the bed to rest. I must have fallen asleep. When I awoke, Sandra had returned to the house, and I'd already been vomiting. I realized that I must have been unsuccessfully trying to change the tire when the heavier particles of radioactive dust and dirt began to drop from the sky. Even now I can feel the grit in my hair and on my skin.

"I'd not explained the dangers of radiation to Sandra, how it would penetrate the walls of a house, and how only a foot or two of earth or concrete surrounding a person could prevent them from being poisoned, but she had obviously picked up that information somewhere."

As CC read, he noticed that Sennett's writing had become irregular, with the ink slightly blurred, the surface of the page mottled. Had he been crying? He seemed to be made of stern stuff.

"I awoke again in the evening, a little stronger, and discovered that Sandra had remained there with me. I insisted she go back to the cave. She made fun of me, but it was with that affection that said we could love one another and still disagree. She said that she would go if I went with her, but when she tried to help me off the bed, I just didn't have the strength to walk. Even a strapping woman would have had trouble supporting my weight, and in spite of her determination my little wife couldn't carry me.

"I finally convinced her to return to the cave for Sarah's sake, and told her I'd be along as soon as I recovered from whatever 'bug' I'd picked up. I had vomited again, and I was afraid she'd notice that there was blood in the pail. I felt a little better after being sick, but knew I was badly dehydrated and hemorrhaging, and that my faculties would soon begin to fail me.

"Sandy tried to lighten the atmosphere by joking with me. She said she'd been missing me, and wanted...*to go out behind the barn with me,* a joke we shared from the early years of our marriage. She stood there staring at me, tears in her eyes, torn between two people she loved, her husband and her granddaughter. And suddenly I knew that she wasn't fooled at all. I tried to make light of it, to act as though everything would be fine, but I'm not much of an actor, and I could never fool Sandy anyway. Besides, she's the one who had excelled in the first-aid courses. She knew the truth.

"I was unable to hide the tears in my eyes. I realized that she might be made ill by any radioactive dust clinging to my hair and clothes, but she put her arms around me.

"Joseph Sennett," she whispered. "Don't you dare cry. If you know something I don't, I'd be mighty surprised. And if it's time for us to part company, then we needn't regret it, for we've shared a lot of good years together." She bit her lip, then said with assurance, "Besides, we'll spend eternity together in heaven."

"Sandra wasn't given to light conversation. She communicated her feelings through her actions, and through some indefinable quality which never failed to reveal her frame of mind. The effort she took to encourage me indicated her concern, for she was obviously burning off the last of her own physical reserves. In spite of the realization that she might also become ill, she still had the capacity to make me laugh.

"We'd shared so much together. No man could have had a better wife or helpmate. There had been times when I must have caused her to age a year in a single day, but that was forgotten now. And if we were to part company for a time, we were both confident that we would ultimately be reunited in God's presence.

"Sandra shifted on the bed by my side, gave me a quick squeeze, and rubbed her nose against mine. Then she whispered, *The Lord be between thee and me while we are apart, one from another, my darling saint Joseph*. For a moment, I was too choked up to respond. Then I whispered, *Amen*. She kissed me lightly on the lips, turned, and fled the house.

His writing had become sloppier, but his thoughts were still clearly expressed.

"It's hard to write a diary like this. You tend to write to impress potential readers, rather than to reflect your true beliefs. It's a lot like praying. We tend to recite our thoughts or speak about God rather than speaking our thoughts and feelings to God. We're born showmen. It takes a lot of time in prayer to cut through all our rubbish."

There was some scribbling on the page. Then he wrote, "I'm too weak to write much more. It all seems so futile. At this moment, I believe more in the idea that our fate has been determined by God's natural laws than in the possibility of His intercession to override those laws for our benefit. After all, the Bible says, '...He causes His sun to rise on the evil and the good, and sends rain on the righteous and the unrighteous.' We allowed our nation to pass the tipping point, and as a result God permitted a world gone mad to pretty much destroy itself."

That was the last entry for that date, and the bottom of the page was stained an ugly brown. CC was careful not to touch the spot, though he felt he probably had nothing to fear from dried vomit. He stopped reading.

Scratch a preacher and you'll get a sermon, he thought wryly. Then he felt ashamed. *America had needed many more such preach-*

ers and sermons, he thought, *and I should have been helping to deliver them.*

He felt as though ice water had been poured over his head. The door of remembrance was again momentarily cracked open, and he knew, for just an instant, who Joseph Sennett was. Not simply who he was. He was certain that he had known Joseph Sennett, but for some reason he could not deal with that realization either. His entire being reacted with stomach-wrenching shock. And then the thread of the memory was gone, and he simply didn't care. He needed to remember, but he wanted even more to avoid remembering. CC sat very still, eyes closed, trying not to think.

After a while, he went to the bookcase and took down a scrapbook. The first was filled with newspaper articles about Sennett's battle to make a nation mighty by making it moral. That had been his slogan, "Might through Morality." The second scrapbook contained pictures and articles about their son, Joseph Sennett. Again, CC was swept with waves of remembrance and foreboding. He dropped the scrapbook on the table by his chair, and his hands returned unbidden to the diary.

CC turned to the last of the entries.

"Vomiting blood... It's the third time I've cried in forty years of marriage — once for young Joseph, once at the end of my ministry, and now, finally, for Sandra and Sarah."

Your ministry hasn't ended, CC thought. You are ministering to me, right now!

The dying man left several more blank pages. The last entry was erratic, the words scrolling diagonally across the page, nearly illegible, the characters growing successively larger in size, the poor spelling and grammar making it almost illegible.

"Hair falling out...can't seem to concen... can't concentrate. Going soon. The dog has returned from the cave. Maybe Sandra sent him.

Live, Sandy! Please live!

"Seems important to write this... What use? Without Sandy, nothing matters."

Then he seemed to rally.

"Poor Sarah. Animals will die without food. Sandra and I shared a good life, except Joseph. Why, Joseph?"

His last words were a plaintive cry.

"Please God, let me be with Sandra."

CC closed the book, and set it on the desk. *I'm too tired,* he thought. He rubbed his eyes to clear his vision, but he discovered that it was his tears that had blurred the words on the page.

His thoughts were interrupted by the screech of a fire alarm, and he looked around startled, trying to comprehend what was going on.

Little Sarah sat up in her bed, a look of terror on her face.

Invaders

The Sennett Farm

June 12th, 1:40 a.m.

He did a quick circuit of the front room, and could smell no smoke nor see any evidence of a fire. "What is it, honey?" he asked her. "Why is there an alarm?"

"Grandpa called it his *spy alarm*," she shouted. CC was struck by the fact that she looked very frightened.

"There's someone coming up the lane from the bridge." Even as she spoke, she had made her way across the room to an old-fashioned entertainment center, and opened two doors. CC was surprised to discover that had hidden a flat panel TV screen.

"That won't work, Sarah," wondering why she'd want to turn on the television set. Then he added, "All the TV stations are off the air."

"It's not to watch TV," she replied, as she pushed the *ON* button.

It took about thirty seconds for the system to warm sufficiently, and then CC was surprised to see the large screen divided into six separate windows, two rows of three, all in a weird greenish light. It took him a moment to realize that he was viewing the output from a number of security cameras, obviously placed in strategic places around the perimeter of the farm.

Four of the screens showed just trees, fields, and fences, but two displayed groups of uniformed men. Again it took him a moment to understand that he was looking at the same group of men from two widely separated surveillance cameras. They were all carrying weapons, and walking slowly up a lane beneath tall pines. CC put his finger on that screen.

"Do you know where this is," he asked.

"Sure. It's just down the lane by the bridge."

"So those men are coming here?"

"I think so." She looked about to cry.

He didn't know why, but CC grabbed Sennett's diary and the scrapbook, and slipped them into her backpack. Then he ran to the kitchen closet and pulled the circuit breaker, putting the entire house in darkness. Settling Sarah's backpack over his shoulders, he scooped her up in his arms. Then he extinguished the lights, stumbled through the living area into Sennett's bedroom, and made his way out the back door. He'd just reached the trees that hid the pathway to the underground barn when he saw a flashlight waving in the darkness, and overheard someone shouting.

"Hey, sarge. Are you sure there's someone here?"

"No. They just wanted us to check it out."

"Are we supposed to burn it?"

"It depends. I was told not to enter the building, so that means no looting."

There were a few curses, but the non-com evidently had his men under control.

"I'm to report in, and they'll give us our orders. They may want to use it this place for something."

"Okay, got it!"

From the moment that he'd pointed at the soldiers on the TV screen, to the time they'd somehow made their way into the tunnel, Sarah hadn't said a word. Now, in pitch darkness, she offered, "I have a little flashlight in my pocket."

"Don't light it yet."

"I won't. Set me down, and I'll lead the way back to the gate. I don't think they'll see the light from there."

CC's smile, though unseen in the darkness, was revealed in his next words. "Wonderful idea, Sarah. You lead the way."

When she finally turned on her flashlight, he was surprised to see the little six-year old run to a circuit box on the wall and open the lid.

"What are you doing, Sarah?"

Without answering, she pulled down a lever.

"Why did you do that?" he asked, his anger obvious even to the child.

"I just turned off the lights to the house," she answered. "Now, even if they turn the switches back on in the closet, nothing will happen."

Well, that little girl's got presence of mind. I didn't think of that. Now they'll never know that we were watching them on closed-circuit TV, unless of course they open the refrigerator and find cold foods. Then they'll know there was power, but maybe still conclude that the place is abandoned. Thank God I didn't light a fire tonight.

The animals were asleep when they entered the cave, and they made their way carefully across the makeshift barn toward the ledge. He knelt down, took one of the acetylene head lamps from the tack chest, filled it with stones and water, and lit it. He didn't want to tell her the bad news, but knew that he couldn't keep it from her much longer.

"Well, honey, we're stuck."

"What do you mean?"

He didn't want to upset her by admitting that he'd probably brought her to a dead end. If the soldiers were to find their way into the tunnel, they'd find the animals and, sooner or later, they'd catch up with them.

"I'm afraid we're trapped in here. The only way out is back to the farm, and then the soldiers would see us. I don't know where to go."

"Well," she answered matter-of-factly, "we can go down to the dam, but I don't like it there. It's damp and cold and very noisy."

"You know how to get to the dam?"

"Of course, silly!" Then she mused, "We could go up the river from the dam, and out the back of the mountain. It's really pretty there."

He was astonished. "You could find that?"

"Yes, but it's a long walk, and I'm kinda tired."

"Well, maybe we could rest here a little while, then go on."

"Why don't we just go to your motor home?"

He was speechless.

"You don't mean that you know where the motor home is?"

"You said that you drove it into the caverns, right?"

"Yes."

"Then it has to be in the big room over in the corner of the valley, and there's only one tunnel that you could have driven it into that would be big enough."

"And you can find it?"

"Sure."

His mind reeled.

"Really?"

At first she'd been answering sort of off-handedly, almost indifferently, but now it was as though he were questioning her integrity or her intelligence.

"Of course I can, silly! I've been there plenty of times." She sighed dramatically. "Grandpa used to joke that some families would take their picnics and go on outings, but almost every week we'd take our picnic and go on an inning." She laughed. "He said we were spelunkers."

"And you don't worry about falling in a hole or some-thing?"

"No, silly. I know the safe ways."

"You really know how to get to the motor home from here?"

She didn't deign to answer him, but instead, turned to-ward the back of the cave. She turned out the lights in the cave, then led CC right past the ledge where he'd met her and her grandmother, the ledge from which he'd made his way to the dam and waterwheel. She went another ten yards beyond and, in the shadow of a protruding wall, slipped through a gap, and disappeared.

He had to kneel down, remove the backpack, shove it through the hole before him, then crawl through the opening. He found her in a room about the size of a bedroom, tapping her foot in impatience, but before he could say anything, she turned a corner and disappeared from sight. He picked up her backpack and hurried after her.

Home Again

From Farm to motor home

June 12th, 8:50 a.m.

CC was amazed that the child had led him unerringly to the motor home in less than thirty minutes. Upon their arrival, Sarah had shown little interest in her surroundings and had immediately gone to bed.

The next morning was warm, with clear skies, but he and Sarah could not risk going outside to cross the valley, so instead made their way back through the caverns to the farm. He was afraid that he'd find a contingent of troops occupying the property, but instead wound up holding a sobbing, broken-hearted youngster in his arms. Her home had indeed been burned to the ground.

He was profoundly shaken to imagine that beautiful little cottage, with all its contents, had been destroyed for no reason. Something inside him seemed to twist at the scene.

Don't these looters realize how much wealth is represented in a single house, and how much money, material, labor, skill and love goes into building one?

The two of them lay hidden in the cedars for nearly an hour as tendrils of smoke rose lazily from the ruins, and he couldn't comprehend why he felt such horror from staring at the charred remains. When he was reasonably certain that none of the soldiers had remained behind, he crept across the field to check the barn. Although the looters had thrown the leather harnesses and some of the tools onto the floor, it was generally undamaged. Why, he wondered, did they burn the house and leave the barn?

He returned to the cave to milk the cow, but found that her calf had the task well under control. The mother goats were nursing their new-born kids as well, and were no longer a burden to him. He wanted to move the animals out into their respective pastures and pens, but dared not because the soldiers might return, or a helicopter might fly over, and the animals would be discovered. They couldn't keep the animals in the cavern much longer, so he told Sarah that they'd probably have to set them free to run wild in the valley.

She wisely suggested that they wait a day or so, then drive the cow, horses, sheep and goats across the valley to some overgrown but fenced pastures that were between the north cliffs and the woods where they would still be penned, but not apt to be seen. CC immediately agreed. She also took him to the barn and showed him a couple of poultry cages. They could, she pointed out, load the poultry into the cages, put them in the back of the pickup truck, and take them across the valley where they could build a new coop. This sounded like good advice too, and they immediately set about the work.

CC had already considered the enormous risk he had taken by remaining so long at the farm. Their escape had been a very close thing and he hated to think what might have happened if it hadn't been for that little girl's cool thinking. He was determined not to be caught sleeping again.

Sarah had wasted no time in advising CC of the dog's proper name, and Baron it was. He smiled. *Everything should be settled that easily.*

They waited until dusk. Then CC took Sarah by the hand, and with Baron barking at the feet of the occasional errant animal, they drove the animals back across the valley toward his cave.

Scraps of a Boy's Life

Joseph Sennett's Scrapbook

June 14th, 7 p.m.

The unremitting labor made the days pass quickly, but CC came to love his too-short evenings together with Sarah. On one particular night she was sounding out the words from a children's book while he continued thumbing through the diary and scrapbook he'd had the presence of mind to salvage from the Sennett house. He thought again of the terrible waste represented by the destruction of the lovely little cottage and its contents.

CC picked up the scrapbook with the clippings and notes that dealt with Sennett's son. The first few pages contained the predictable baby pictures, crayon scribblings, and the photo of the child with his first bike. As might be expected, the elementary report cards boasted straight A's in academic work as well as deportment. There were photos of a boy in football uniform, and in coat and tie as president of his junior high student council. There was even a picture of him with a pretty girl, both in formal wear.

The remainder of the book's pages were blank, but a thick manilla envelope was stuffed inside the back cover. CC shook out the contents and began to sort through them. They dealt with the boy's passage from childhood through adolescence. CC wondered why they had not been pasted into the book until he looked them over more carefully.

A brief newspaper article dealt with teen-age vandalism in the community, and told of the arrest of three boys who were subsequently placed on probation, but whose names were withheld because of their status as youthful offenders.

One editorial attacked wanton violence in school sports, and singled out Joseph Sennett, the son of a prominent clergyman, who was accused off seriously injuring opponents on the soccer field. The teen had received warnings from the referees and had been removed from several games, but he continued to use a dangerous slide kick to disable key opposing players. The writer argued that "...something must to be done about boys like him." He also remarked that the boy was "...typical of Christians of this era who don't care who they hurt in promoting themselves."

CC was unable to understand what the writer meant by that slur, but was not displeased with the comment that, "The son, like his father, wears a silver cross on his jersey during games." CC remembered something about the cross. There'd been a civil liberties lawsuit, and a court ruled that players and fans could no longer wear religious symbols in public. The soccer star then quit the team.

CC picked up the next paper, a "Notice of Suspension." It stated that, "Joseph Sennett has been suspended from school for three days for cheating on an examination." It required that he make an appointment with the principal, and must be accompanied by both parents to seek reinstatement.

The next item was a letter from the school principal, still in its original envelope. It had been sent by certified mail, return receipt requested, about a week after the suspension notice. It informed the Sennetts that their son had been truant from school for five days, and asked them why they had not returned to the school with him following his three-day suspension.

On the back of the principal's letter, Sennett had scribbled some notes.

"My wife was almost too old to bare children by the time Joseph arrived on the scene. We were already in our forties. We were so thrilled that the Lord had finally answered our prayers, and it never occurred to us that all too soon we would be dealing with a difficult teenager. I was close to sixty and at the peak of my ministry when he entered high school. These increased burdens coincided with a natural decline in our energies."

Leafing through the clippings, CC found a copy of a newspaper interview. As he read through it, he realized why he'd suffered a sense of foreboding when he first heard the Sennett name. He scanned the article in which the reporter interviewed the boy's father. The writer wove a fascinating fable of a troubled son's moral odyssey. Her interview with the boy's father was brutal.

"Reverend Sennett. The courts have had your son taken away from you to protect him from your abuse. Any comment?"

"We did not abuse our son."

"Come now, Mr. Sennett. I saw a photo of a facial bruise."

"I did not strike my son on the face. Ever!"

"Would you like to tell your side of the story?"

"I'm advised by counsel to wait until the trial is over."

"Oh, come now, Reverend, is it really necessary to stonewall?"

"I am not stonewalling, and I'll say this much. It's true that I tried to discipline him; but I never abused him. Caught in a lie, my son admitted a theft, and I spanked him...but only on the buttocks. In reaction, he ran away. Evidently, he walked into town. Somehow he got together with a welfare worker, and she fabricated a tale that resulted in our son being taken from us."

The reporter left her question and answer format here, and challenged him.

"Surely you're not implying that an underpaid, over-worked, dedicated social servant is guilty of improper conduct?"

"I am not implying any such thing. I am stating that an overpaid, underworked, power-hungry socialist manipulated the facts in order to harm her political enemies."

Sennett did his case no good when he suggested to the reporter that she herself should do more research, and then went blithely on, telling a story that would never reach the public.

"Those people were only too happy to cast me and my ministry in a bad light. I didn't strike our son's face, but they succeeded in blaming it on me. One consequence of the notoriety was that our ministry died."

The reporter commented in her article, "Mr. Sennett can scarcely blame the timely demise of his so-called ministry on the child protection agency or the respected governor of one of our largest states." She concluded her article with, "The elder Sennett was charged with a felony for child abuse, but was somehow able to avoid jail time." She didn't add that the jury had found him innocent, nor that the teen was manipulated into becoming the ward of the governor of New York.

CC found a letter that young Joseph had secretly written to his father just five years earlier. In that letter he confessed that he and a young woman who served as a maid in the governor's mansion had engaged in an affair. It was one of the few times in his young life that the boy admitted to anything. He told his father how, at seventeen, he and the young woman had fallen in love.

Over time, Joseph's father had been able to work out the truth. He had scribbled notes on several scraps of paper, and stapled those findings to his son's letter.

When the governor's staff uncovered the affair, and it was discovered that the maid was pregnant, the governor decided to do everything possible to avoid any embarrassment to himself. When he told the maid that he would never allow Joseph to marry her, and she adamantly refused to have an abortion, he decided to railroad her.

In order to frighten her, he had her jailed overnight. Then, since she was a few months older than Joseph, and since she had just turned eighteen and was legally an adult, the governor warned that he would have her charged with statutory rape. Pregnant, and threatened with five years in prison, the frightened girl accepted the governor's offer for a suspended sentence in return for pleading guilty to a lesser charge and leaving the state.

"Our son didn't learn about her pregnancy for several years, nor why she really disappeared. Instead, he was given a note that she was forced to write in which she stated that she didn't love him and that she was leaving New York to get away from him. She disappeared, and he could find no one who would tell him anything more."

Several years later, the broken-hearted young man learned the truth from one of the governor's staff members.

Even then, he didn't get the entire truth. He was told that she and the baby died during childbirth.

In truth, since she had no family of her own, Joseph's parents invited her into their home and the young woman had gone to live with them, ironically staying in their son's old bedroom.

"As I look back," the elder Sennett's notes continued, "I realize that Joseph spent his early years struggling with moral questions. It took me a long time before I came to understand the disillusionment that many preacher's kids suffer for the sacrifices their parents willingly undertake, and the verbal abuse they often suffer at the hands of others — even professing Christians. Why a P.K. should be held to a higher standard is something I will never understand.

"After all, it's the parents who make the decision to leave all and follow Christ. The children are not offered the same option. It might be many years, if ever, that a preacher's children realize that they have been provided with many unique opportunities and blessings that other children could never even dream of. And I believe that Joseph was one of those who lost sight of the compensations he received from God as a preacher's kid.

"Was it God who made these demands on him, or was it me? Every preacher, every parent, should ask himself that question? *Does my child have to pay a price for the lifework I have chosen?* It seems obvious that all children should accommodate themselves to some degree to their parent's careers, for it is the source of the family's survival, and in an ideal world, would be the parent's response to God's calling. Some parents, however, focus themselves on their careers to the exclusion of all else, often ignoring and even neglecting their children.

"Certainly we cannot completely divorce our children from our work. They should understand something about what we do, and even take pride in it. But beyond doing their household chores, their responsibilities should encompass their preparation for life, their schooling, their support of the family's home life and structure, and their personal relationship with God, family, and community.

"Our children should certainly have regular family tasks assigned them that are commensurate with their abilities and maturity. But any burdens involving in our careers should be limited to whatever is required to help the family survive, and throughout they should receive our love and praise. Any labor on their parts should help them mature and develop character. In Joseph's case, he found himself the object of verbal abuse by teachers and peers because of his parent's ministries.

"Unfortunately, after Joseph was taken from us, he wound up doing dirty jobs for cynical, avaricious, self-serving people who became rich by exploiting others. As our son passed through these trials, the governor introduced him to the causes he supported, and they became very important to the boy. They seemed socially significant, glamorous, even noble — and they were very lucrative. As time passed, however, Joseph became disillusioned.

It must have been about that time that he realized how venial and corrupt these people were, and he made a resolution to be different, to be the hammer of God, to turn things around. He would appear to serve them while finding ways to hurt them, and one way to hurt them was to embarrass them. So Joseph behaved in ways that embarrassed his stepfather.

"As the governor grew weary of covering up repeatedly for Joseph's indiscretions, he sought to keep the teen out of the limelight. He sent Joseph to the state university, but the teen didn't spend much time in classes. When Joseph was eighteen, his adoptive parent finally tried to throw him out of the governor's mansion because he had become a political liability. Those shrewd politicians never imagined that Joseph had been gathering hard evidence of his step-father's criminal behavior, but when they tried to warn him off, they learned that he had been so clever in handling the evidence that they dared not threaten him.

"Nor did they any longer feel safe in incorporating him into their affairs, so they instead gave him money to travel around the world for a year. That would, they were sure, keep him busy until his stepfather could win his last term in office.

"Joseph did indeed leave the country, but then they lost track of him. There was some indication that he'd returned to the USA after just just a couple of weeks, but since he remained out of sight and caused them no trouble, they didn't care. In fact, a friend of ours once told us that he thought he saw Joseph hunting on a large forested parcel that we own about twenty miles northwest of Hidden Valley.

"As it turned out, Joseph was not a prodigal, especially when it came to handling money. He invested his income carefully, following the best advice. He was very careful, and though he appeared to live high, he made his money grow."

"Joseph was our only child, and very precious to both of us. His mother never accused me of being the cause of his being snatched from us. And I never told her that I had received just one other letter from Joseph during all these years. His words broke my heart, and I hid the letter. On the basis of that letter, and of all of the things I have read and heard, I was forced to draw some conclusions.

"Looking back through the years, I realized that he had always loved us, and that he had cried out for our attention, for our appreciation and our affection, but like too many preachers, I was so busy trying to save a lost and dying world that I lost the battle for the one soul for which God had given me responsibility.

"Our son tried to be different for two reasons. He wanted to get our attention, and he wanted us to appreciate his success at being something more than a rubber stamp of his father. It was ironic, for it would have taken little effort to outdo me.

"Joseph was the tragic product, not just of an over-worked preacher-father, but of a very corrupt society. I think that he was reacting to two things. First, he was crushed because, when he played life straight, he was mistreated. Second, he wanted to succeed at any price. He wanted this success to win our respect and love. He simply never had the spiritual maturity to understand the real issues and to comprehend that we had always loved him.

"Perhaps, in the presumptuous power of youth, our son determined to use his strength to meet the evils of his age and prevail against them, but he was not willing or able to pay the high price. He found that, all too often, there is no organized, dedicated enemy. People simply appear to act together in unison because they are motivated by fear or greed or some other temptations.

"He could not cope with the reality of sin. In Joseph's opinion, everyone is sooner or later ground down by their circumstances and they ultimately yield themselves to temptation. They become part of the lowest common denominator, as surely as water flows downhill to gather in a noisome swamp.

"Joseph's determination to stand above the crowd, his enormous ambition to be a somebody, soon transformed itself into a cynical resolve to manipulate the crowd, to bend it to his will for his own self-interests. Like de Gaulle, he reasoned that one cannot make an omelet without breaking a few eggs. His motto became, *The end justifies the means!* He made Machiavelli his hero.

"Because he espoused superior motives, he somehow supposed that his own character was not subject to the same rules as others. He decided that he would become so powerful that he would be able to use, and later discard, the hypocrites. He was determined to bend them to his superior will. Then he would crush them and, standing alone, take his proper, well-earned place in society, leading the less able and the less dedicated.

"He never seemed to realize that he was following the same path of self-delusion that legions of others had been paving with the bricks of cynicism and mortar of despite since the beginning of time.

"Judgment yielded to ambition. Pride overcame caution. Integrity surrendered to expediency. Our son became slave to the very philosophy he abhorred. He too became a hypocrite!

"He soon found himself entangled in a clumsy web of his own weaving. But webs are for spiders, and unlike a spider, our son was not designed to weave webs, nor to make his home in a web, nor to hunt his prey therein. For, as a child, and at his mother's knee, he had heard the gospel which was able to make him wise unto salvation through faith which is in Christ Jesus. And that reality, carved deep into the clay of his being, brought pangs of conscience at the most inconvenient moments."

CC felt compelled to continue his reading.

"Once, in a moment of unusual clairvoyance, Joseph confessed that he was the one that made the choices for which he blamed me. As with many men of great pride, he also suffered from a profound sense of insecurity and inferiority. He would rise to giddy heights of self-glory, then plunge to depths of hideous despair and self-loathing.

"He sought to remove this grain of truth, this cutting condemnation, by coating it with a veneer of double delusion. After his sweetheart inexplicably disappeared from the governor's mansion, it was rumored that he developed a curious contempt for the innocent girls he seduced, somehow balancing his attitude with the fallacious argument that he was doing them a favor by jilting them in order to save them from an unhappy relationship. It was an act he was said to consider most noble.

His reputation, however, exceed reality. I could find no evidence of Joseph's having had a single illicit affair apart from the one, and I suspect that the rumors were the work of the governor's staff, determined to undermine him.

"Apart from that, however, I believe that he somehow contrived to accumulate scores of contradictory values in the closets of his mind, but was careful to open only one door at a time to examine its contents. For if he had dragged everything out at once, his elaborate rationales would soon be exposed as a crazy quilt confusion of contradictions that might well drive him mad.

"At his sixteenth birthday party, just before we had our final argument, someone asked him why he never attended our church. He responded, *It's not because of my father. No. If I go to church, any church, I'll find out how bad I am. And if I find out how bad I am, then I'll have to change. And I don't want to change.*

"He was not being flippant. He was absolutely serious. And he later succored himself with the argument that his ultimate but indistinct goal of benefiting mankind would somehow justify whatever steps were necessary to attain his dubious ends. So, with one simple shift in values, our son appeared to become the epitome of the cynical, avaricious, self-serving people whom he had dedicated himself to root out and destroy.

"In spite of the fact that I'd tried to keep the truth from his mother; I was too blind to realize that she would inevitably uncover them for herself, and would try to keep those very same facts from me. We were both broken-hearted.

"I could not free myself from a terrible sense of failure and loss, but I also realized that all of us reach a stage in life when we must take responsibility for our own actions. We may overlook the fact that one day each of us must stand before God to answer for our own faith and conduct, but Joseph knew the truth, and he was very bright. He was therefore culpable. I pray that our son will be prepared to bear that eternal burden before it's too late."

CC set the open book down on the sofa, and went to the stove to pour himself a cup of coffee, sweetening it with honey and the rich cream from the Jersey he was milking daily. Sadly, they used only a quart or so of the surplus the cow provided, and rarely more than four of the dozens of eggs the hens produced. *It's a pity,* he thought. *There are multitudes out there starving to death for want of a single egg or a glass of milk.*

He went to stand by the hearth, soaking up the heat and light as though they could dispel his icy feelings of disquiet. Then he returned to the scrapbook to finish reading the account of a father's broken dreams.

"Joseph's ambitions were not simple. For as long as I can remember, he appeared to want all the money he could get his hands on, and all the power and pleasure he could buy with it. It was a vicious downward spiral. The more money he got, the more power he bought. And that increasing power required more money.

"And his dubious pleasures saw him sliding into a moral abyss which produced increasing pain and disillusionment rather than satisfaction or growth. He didn't care how he accumulated money as long as he was able to keep his name fairly clean and managed to remain out of court.

"Through the years, the press had begun to question what role he really played in liberal political circles. He hadn't reached his twenties before they began to categorize him as a shady businessman and a special operator for two major public-sector unions, but after he won a huge liable suit from a New York tabloid, the critics backed off. After a while, they ignored him completely.

"When as a teenager Joseph lied at the bidding of the social service people, it was a symptom of his problems, not the cause. Yes, he ruined his own life, but we had our part, and it all contributed to the death of our ministry. Perhaps that was God's judgment on all of us. I don't know anymore.

"So my wife and I moved here. This little valley has been in my family for over two hundred years. We had a little cash left, and we loved the idea of homesteading. It was a welcome relief to be away from those fair-weather friends who ignored and even abused us when we needed them most. On the other hand, we really missed the zealous and enthusiastic young Christians who were always eager to yield themselves to the service of the Lord.

"We were here only a few months when the state widened the highway along the mountain, and barred us from any longer having our driveway exit out onto it. It was patently illegal, but they got away with it, and that effectively isolated us from the world. Oddly, we did not mind. We became twentieth-century hermits."

CC slipped the materials back in the envelope. He now knew more about Joseph Sennett and his father than he knew about himself.

He started washing up, and the noise awoke Sarah. She sensed his somber attitude and strove to cheer him up. They had breakfast together. He couldn't remember what they ate, but it was wonderful to have her here with him. He checked the radiation count. Then they spent the morning together, looking after the needs of the animals.

Lust for Power

Leaving Sarah Behind

June 16th, 8:30 p.m.

CC's compulsion to create a reliable electrical generation system drove him to attempt things for which he knew he had neither sufficient resourcefulness nor strength. It was easy enough to make a list of items he would need, and to create a plan to achieve his goals, but quite another thing to actually undertake such an ambitious and probably futile project.

For one thing, it would require that he leave the valley and, of far greater concern, to leave Sarah alone. Such a trip would be far too dangerous to take her along. He would have to risk traveling back to the hospital, secure the generator and other necessary equipment, and somehow return undetected.

And the thought of leaving this newfound security, regardless of how tenuous it might actually be, frightened him. What's more, if something happened to him, Sarah would not survive. He couldn't bring himself to use the word, "die." The two of them had already forged a strong bond of trust, and apart from the fact that she helped satisfy his craving for companionship and affection, he had come to think of this little girl as his own daughter and he did not want any harm to come to her.

Nonetheless, one sparkling evening while looking at Sennett's old pickup truck, he plucked up his resolve and made the decision to leave the following morning. He spent a good deal of the evening checking out the decrepit truck, loading it with emergency supplies and preparing for the trip. Then he sat for an hour with Sarah, talking about their future together and praying with her. When he started to give instructions for her welfare during his absence, she assured him in no uncertain terms that she knew there was enough canned food available to last her for a good long time.

"And I will feed the chickens, gather the eggs, and milk the cow every day," she'd assured him. CC stifled a laugh, for he knew that her tiny hands were only adequate to get a little milk from the cow, but fortunately, the nursing calf would make up for the child's shortcomings.

He had moved two cow stanchions from Sennett's barn, setting them up in the mouth of the cave nearest the rattlesnake's nest. Since the Chinese didn't fly their planes after dark, one bright night he burned off the area where the rattlesnakes nested, and the next day searched the area for any reptiles that hadn't been driven off by the fire. After that, he and Sarah built a chicken coop just inside the cave.

The animals were free to wander through the woods and over the meadow during the day, and he'd even fenced off the portion of the meadow so that the livestock would otherwise be in danger of falling into the deep crevices. At night the animals were secured behind a gate that he'd erected across the mouth of the cave, similar to the one that Sennett had erected in his underground barn.

Although he was hesitant to permit Sarah to go outside to complete these chores, he realized that she had a mind of her own and there was probably no stopping her. It was only after they'd prayed together that she revealed her true concerns.

"CC?" she appealed, with tears in her eyes. "Do you really have to go?"

He took her in his arms, asking himself the same question for the tenth time. "Yes, honey, I think that I do. You see, we don't know what's happening out there, and it's important that we try to find out."

"Out where?"

"Out in the rest of the world, honey. And it's not just for our own sakes, but because we might be able to help someone else."

Tears welled up, and she turned away to hide them. In a small voice she said, "I know there are people in trouble, but what about me? I'm so little. And I was alone taking care of grandma for a long time too." She turned to him, tears running down her cheeks. "What if you don't come back? What will I do?" She wiped the back of her hand across her nose, and he handed her a tissue.

He started to laugh. She looked up at him with an indignant expression. Pushing him away, she put her hands on her hips and demanded, "What's so funny?"

"Nothing, Sarah." He was unsuccessful in conquering his smile. "Well, actually, you are."

"I'm funny?"

"Not in the way you think." He put his arms around her and drew her to him. "You know what?"

"What?" she asked, annoyance mixed with curiosity.

"You're a little survivor."

"Huh!"

He looked at her, appraising her, as though seeing something in her that he hadn't noticed before. "Yes, you're a real survivor." Then he did laugh. "And you know what else?"

"What?"

"I'm not even sure which of us is in charge here." At that, she tried to look indignant, but he grinned and said, "Somehow I suspect it's you." With that, she laughed too, and hugged him tight.

Then he turned serious. "I'll be back, Sarah. I promise." He had no idea how he could make good on such a rash promise, but it seemed to reassure her, and her confidence in him made him realize that he meant what he said. He would be back, or he'd die trying.

Still, she persisted. "Can't you stay here? We'll be happy as long as we're together."

"No Sarah, I can't stay here." He'd made it a habit never to talk down to her. "We have to establish a certain way of life which we can maintain for a long time. I want that electrical generator. We need a heating system that will reliably provide for us for many years. One that will free us from dangerous and difficult labor. One that will guarantee us some free time." He didn't add that he might not always be able to pro-vide firewood and food because he might not always be there.

She didn't understand all that he said, but he was able to convince her of the importance of his journey. Finally she nodded her head in resignation, her eyes shiny with tears but her lips tight with determination.

He picked her up and swung her in a circle, singing her a children's song. She giggled, snuffling through her tears, and he groped for another tissue to wipe her nose. Life had taken on an entirely new dimension for him, and at that moment he felt very important and very much needed. Then, for an instant, the faces of two other children inexplicably flashed across his mind, and the shock almost caused him to drop her. *Who were they?* he wondered? *What do they have to do with me?*

An unusually sensitive child, she immediately picked up on the change in his demeanor. "What's wrong, CC?"

"Nothing, honey. I was just thinking of some other children."

"Who?"

"Oh, I don't know. Just children in general."

"Oh," she replied in a voice that betrayed her doubt.

He said prayers with her before putting her to bed in the cave, and then stayed nearby until he was certain she was fast asleep, as he'd promised. He was tired when he arose at four, but was still determined to make the trip. When he awoke her to say "goodbye," she gave him a little hug and went right back to sleep. Then he was off into the darkness and the pre-morning chill to start the old truck.

Black River Revisited

Medical Center

Deep River Junction, Vermont

June 17th, 6:20 a.m.

Sennett's old pickup had one virtue, a good muffler, so as CC bounced along the rough track down the canyon he was confident that it was unlikely to be heard by anyone. It was the false dawn — the sun wouldn't actually rise until about 7 a.m., but he was able to follow the log road without using the headlights. Reaching the upper end of the bottleneck, he left the truck idling while he reconnoitered the entry to make certain there was no traffic on the highway.

When he pulled the truck out from beneath the evergreens, he turned to the right, and began climbing the hill toward Deep River Junction. Thirty miles of tense but uneventful driving brought him to the edge of town. He pulled the truck in behind an old service station so that he could get out and look around.

After he'd peered down the highway and listened for any tell-tale sounds, CC drove slowly around the west side of the small city, keeping the old truck moving as quietly as possible. When he did hear truck engines roaring and transmissions being punished in the center of the town, he turned away and continued around the perimeter toward the hospital.

This furious activity heightened his suspicion about the radio reports he'd heard, declaring this town to be officially off limits. He was not surprised. This abandoned and now uncontaminated area was a treasure trove of equipment and consumer goods to those who were creating their little fiefdoms in the New England mountains. They were probably stripping the town bare of everything of value.

Not that I didn't get my share, he thought with mixed feelings. *I just hope the generator is still here, and that I can get it out of town without being caught.*

He knew he was drawing near to the hospital long before he reached it, and pulled on a surgical face mask in a futile effort to filter out some of the odor. Warily approaching the facility, he backed the pickup truck to the loading dock that was just a few yards from the generator installation.

A whippoorwill struck a plaintive note as he brushed past the lilacs that overhung the paved walk. Although their perfume was almost overwhelmed by the reek of death, he couldn't help but appreciate the fact that beauty could still exist in a world corrupted by man. And in spite of his feverish desire to get here, load the generator, and get back home, he stopped for a moment to take cuttings of the lilacs that he hoped to plant near the cave portals.

He hurried along the back of the building to the mechanical room, hoping that other scavengers hadn't already pirated the generator. *Maybe*, he thought, *the horrible smell has discouraged the bad guys from coming around to pillage the hospital.* He smiled in relief when he saw that the big machine was still there, just outside the mechanical room. It was housed in its large, bright yellow steel cabinet, and surrounded by a tall chain link fence crowned with razor wire. Large pipes enclosed the cables that ran from the generator to the hospital's electrical center.

The steel door to the generator cabinet had a large decal affixed, warning of the danger of electrocution. CC smiled at the irony. There hadn't been any high voltage electricity passing through those cables in a couple of months. His eyes flicked across the bright yellow cabinet to another decal. "16 KW, 60 Hz Mission Critical Diesel Fueled Generator Set."

I was right! This little country hospital couldn't afford a prime generator set, just something big enough to run emergency systems, but there is no question that the generator will produce far more power than I would require, and it's designed to run for extended periods. That leaves me with three immediate questions. First, can I disconnect the generator from its diesel engine? Second, can I get the generator into the bed of the truck? And, third, will the old truck carry that heavy a load?

The odor was terrible, but not as enervating as the pictures he was drawing in his mind. I must be tired, he thought. I need to concentrate. He leaned back into the dense shrubbery across the sidewalk from the steel access panel, took several shallow breaths, and tried to concentrate on the challenge while avoiding the impulse to be sick.

He had been half listening for anyone who might be moving in the area, but all he heard was the roaring of engines in the distance. He sought to let the ordinary sounds, like the rustling leaves and the buzzing insects fade into the background so that he could pick out anything unusual. He should have begun listening sooner.

He felt the pressure of the gun's muzzle against the back of his neck at the same time that a young and uncertain voice snarled, "Don't move, or I'll shoot."

The Assailant

Medical Center
Deep River Junction, Vermont
June 17th, 6:38 a.m.

He froze, alternately shocked and frightened by the pressure of the gun's muzzle against the base of his skull. Then he found himself trying to assess the danger. It seemed likely that his assailant could and would deliver on his threat. *Why not?* he thought. *This is a lawless society. People are killing one another for little or no reason at all.*

Suddenly the attacker's voice quavered slightly, and the uncertainty made CC realize that he was probably more dangerous because he was also frightened. The pressure of the muzzle relaxed slightly, and his assailant moved to the side. CC stood very still, moving only his eyes, trying to focus on the person standing on his periphery.

He was little more than a boy really, and he moved around just out of reach until he was facing CC. He held a small caliber rifle, an ancient "over and under." One barrel was obviously a 22 caliber, the other a small gauge shotgun.

Doesn't matter, CC realized. *At point-blank range, either would be lethal.*

"What are you doing here?" the boy demanded.

CC strove to remain calm, considering the potentially deadly consequences of a confrontation with a teenager who had, without doubt, been severely traumatized by the war. Recalling the old Proverb, that "...a soft answer turns away wrath," he forced himself to answer in a calm and even voice. "I've come to get that electrical generator." CC had raised his hands above his head, and without lowering them, he tipped his index finger to point toward the cabinet.

The boy glanced across the walk, but kept his weapon trained on CC. "Don't you know it's against the law to take anything from here, or even to be here?"

"What law?"

"What do you mean, 'What law?' Why, the law made by the new government. Everybody's gotta obey it or there'll be..." He hesitated as if searching for an unfamiliar word, and continued rather lamely, as though tasting the unaccustomed syllables, "...or there'll be anarchy."

They stared at one another for a moment longer, then, without changing his posture, the boy seemed to relax slightly, perhaps concluding that CC didn't represent a threat to him, or because he felt he controlled the situation.

"You're not one of them, are you?" It was more of a statement than a question.

"No." CC answered flatly; "I'm not one of them." He raised one eyebrow. "Are you?"

"No!" As in, of course not!

The boy lowered the muzzle a little, and CC surprised himself with an unexpected sigh of relief. He was surprised at the conviction expressed in the boy's next words.

"I think they're just ripping people off, the way everybody's been doing to everybody else since the war started. The way governments always do."

"Governments didn't always rip people off. On very rare occasions, they even represented the citizen's best interests."

"Yeah, on very rare occasions." The boy frowned, an unspoken challenge in his eyes, obviously trying to assess CC's character. The rifle that was now leveled at CC's stomach continued to represent a very real danger. CC was sure the boy was unstable so he continued speaking calmly.

"Well, I agree that this so-called government is clearly dishonest and definitely dangerous, so you've been wise to avoid any contact with them."

The boy did not respond, leaving CC to question whether they'd touched upon any common ground, but the teen's next words were more assuring.

"They don't really care about anybody except them-selves." His voice grew more confident as he warmed to his subject. "They had hundreds of cases of food stacked up where they were loading it into tractor-trailers," tipping his head to point toward the center of the city. When I asked them for something to eat, they made me help load the boxes, but they didn't give me anything, and they even took away the few things I'd brought with me from home. So I ran off when they were taking a beer break. A couple of them came look-ing for me, but I hid. I still can't figure out why they were so mad. They robbed me, I didn't rob them."

In his excitement, he was waving the rifle around.

"Son," CC said, to get his attention. He had to repeat himself more loudly, "Son, be careful that you don't fire that gun. It will bring them running."

The teen stood blank-faced for a moment before he seemed to comprehend CC's warning. Finally he pointed the weapon toward the ground. "It's not even loaded," he said, not in the least embarrassed to make the admission. "I had a beauty of a hunting rifle, but this morning it was taken from me by those guys downtown. "I just found this thing along with a few rounds of ammunition in a garage down the street," and he grinned as he pulled several cartridges from his pocket.

CC found himself clenching his fists as he raised his voice to a dangerous level. "Do you realize how stupid that was?"

The boy stare was blank.

"You threatened me with an empty weapon. I might have killed you, thinking I was acting in self-defense."

The boy's couldn't hide his embarrassment. "You're right, it was stupid. I didn't load it because I didn't want to shoot you. I was always taught that you should never point a gun unless you're ready to shoot it."

"Well," CC responded angrily, you sure got your wires crossed there. "Following that logic, if you weren't ready to shoot me, you shouldn't have pointed the rifle at me."

The boy looked sheepish, his head hanging down, balanced on one foot, the toes of the other twisting back and forth. He hesitated. "Anyway," he said brightly, "I'm not with those guys," again indicating by a tip of his head the direction from which a great roaring came as the convoy of trucks began to move north out of town. Then, betraying his loneliness and insecurity, the boy whispered what seemed almost an appeal, but was really a fatal confession. "I'm not with anybody."

CC appeared not to have heard the remark as he stepped around the boy and used a pair of bolt cutters to remove the padlock from the gate on the chain-link fence. He entered the compound, opened an access hatch, and was engrossed in an examination of the generator set. He was terribly disappointed. It was clear that he'd never be able to disconnect the diesel engine which powered it, and carry off the generator. It was far too big and heavy. The bolt heads were over two inches across, and he'd need a bulldozer-sized socket wrench and a breaker bar at least three feet long. And even if he could break the generator apart from the diesel engine, he knew that his old pickup truck would collapse under its weight.

The boy watched with interest as CC walked back out of the enclosure, his shoulders slumped, his head down.

"What's the matter," he stammered.

CC looked up, surprised, having forgotten the boy's presence in the midst of his own disappointment.

"I'd hoped to remove that generator and take it with me, but it's too big."

The boy nodded in understanding. "Yeah, it is really big, isn't it?"

CC didn't bother responding.

They could still hear truck engines being revved up a few blocks away, and CC realized he didn't dare to try leaving town yet. He decided to look through the basement to see if there was anything else of value he might take back to the valley.

"How'd you expect to turn the driveshaft on that huge generator?" the boy asked.

"I had a way," was all CC would offer.

"But do you really need something that big?"

"Beggars can't be choosers, Son."

"Does that mean you could work with something smaller?"

"Most smaller machines don't generate enough power."

"Well, how about that one," the boy asked innocently, pointing across the lawn toward a small office complex.

"How about what one," CC asked, mildly annoyed at the interruption.

"Over there, by the hedge on the left of the building, with the wheels. Can't you see it?"

And suddenly he did see it, and he couldn't believe his eyes.

He looked around to make certain no one was nearby, then dashed across the lawn to examine the little treasure. It was a 150 kW generator set.

Designed to power small businesses, like the lights and refrigeration units in convenience stores, it was enclosed in its own small cabinet, mounted atop a trailer with two wheels and an ordinary trailer hitch.

He checked the size of the hitch, and found it required a 2" ball. He'd never paid any attention to the hitch on the truck, so he ran back to check the size. He laughed when he discovered that it had three different size balls mounted to the sides of its thick steel shaft. All he had to do was pull a pin, slip the assembly out of its box channel, rotate it, and reinsert it with the correct size on top.

The boy startled him out of his reverie. "Can I help you, mister?"

Working alone and relying on himself for so long, CC had dismissed him from his thoughts.

"If I'd needed to disconnect that big machine over there," he said, pointing toward the big standby unit, "I'd sure have welcomed your help. But this is easy." Then, as an after-thought, "Thanks, anyway. Oh, and thanks for pointing this out to me."

He worked quickly, backing the truck up to the mobile generator set, cranking the jack on the trailer down so that the cup seated over the truck hitch, and securing it. When he heard the sound of an approaching truck, he almost pan-icked. Realizing that he was hidden from the highway by the office building, he just stayed where he was, hoping the driver would pass on by the hospital. He did.

After the truck disappeared up the road, CC put his pickup in low, raced the engine, and found he had to rock it to break the trailer's wheels free from where they'd settled into the ground. Once rolling, the load seemed to tow easily enough. He drew up near the loading dock to the hospital, wondering how much extra weight he could carry in the bed of the pickup.

He pulled open the doors into the hospital basement, and the boy followed him in. As they wandered the short dis-tance down the hall from the utility area, the smell didn't seem as bad as outside, and CC removed his mask. The boy answered a question that had been nagging at CC.

"The radio reported that all the patients were sent home, or loaded on buses and trucks to be taken north. That's why I was here when you arrived. I thought they might have left something behind, some food or blankets or something, and this might be a place I could stay for a while. Now I realize," he added, "that no one could stay here."

Nearly choking on the stench in the air, CC tipped his head to look up at the ceiling. When he looked back, the boy nodded his head in confirmation.

"It was all a lie. The only patients that got out of here were the ones who walked out on their own feet after the at-tacks. The rest are still here."

CC turned to the boy. "The basement has a concrete ceiling. The rest of this old building is just wood frame with brick veneer. The patients didn't stand a chance of surviving the radiation, but even if they had, they would have perished from lack of food and medical care."

At the mention of food, the boy appeared faint. In spite of the horrors of war, the ever-present specter of starvation allowed one's mind to move from the macabre to personal needs in an instant.

"How long has it been since you've eaten?"

"A while."

"When did you last eat?"

"I had an apple yesterday morning."

CC frowned. "Come with me," a hint of impatience in his voice. He led the boy back to the truck, opened a can of pork and beans, and handed him both the can and a plastic spoon. Reaching back onto the truck seat, he added a couple of packets of saltines and a single serving can of fruit juice. For someone on the edge of starvation, too much juice might cause problems.

He'd scarcely turned back toward the building when he noticed that the boy was wolfing everything down. *That might be a good sign,* he thought, *for if he were really starving, he'd eat more slowly.* He reached into his pocket, found what he was looking for, and flipped the boy a candy bar. The lad somehow got a hand free and snatched it out of the air. Then he simply stood there and stared at the wrapping as though it were a rare and precious thing.

"Well, go ahead," CC muttered gruffly. "Eat it."

The boy seemed to hesitate, then asked, "Do you mind if I save it?"

He realized that the boy had never expected to see a candy bar again. And it probably represented a sort of security, not merely something that he could save to eat later, but a food reserve, better than money in the bank, a comfortable link to the past, a symbol of hope for the future.

There was only one response CC could make. "Sure, hang on to it. Why not?" He could answer questions in the interrogative too.

He'd turned back toward the basement when the boy asked, "Mister, where are you going?"

"Well, I'm on a short shopping trip."

"Could you spare some food?"

"Sure. Help yourself."

While the boy rummaged through the cab of the truck, CC went back inside to collect antibiotics and other supplies from the hospital dispensary. He knew he risked the boy's taking his entire food supply, but he was banking on his honesty. And this last trip to a pharmacy was an important one. Anything that might happen in his hidden valley would probably require something more than a band-aid and an aspirin, so he rifled the drug cabinets. Someone had been there since he'd left, and had removed all the amphetamines, but in a locked closet, he found an inoperable refrigerator containing ampoules of morphine and cartons of antibiotics.

These were items that could save lives later on, and were already undoubtedly priceless. He picked up cartons of sutures, individually packed in foil and immersed in jars filled with an antiseptic. He also gathered sponges, clamps, hypodermics, clamps, hemostats, and scalpels, all individually and sanitarily packaged, a treasure trove of items that had so far been overlooked or forgotten by the drug-hungry scavengers. He carefully packed them in well-padded boxes, then stowed them in the pickup under a tarpaulin that he carefully tied down.

He hesitated, uneasy about the amount of time he'd already spent there, wondering whether he dared stay any longer. He realized that it was unlikely that he'd ever return to this place, and he'd better get whatever he could now, so he quickly made his way to the kitchen. Because he'd disposed of the cooked food on the steam tables weeks before, there was little sign of vermin, and the odors were far less offensive here than outside the building.

He pushed through to the storeroom, and began sorting through the cases of the canned goods he found stacked there. He tried to select things that would improve the flavor of the bags of rice and beans he gathered earlier, things that he and Sarah might enjoy, especially fruits, gravies, and sauces. Loading the cases on the dolly, he pushed it back to the truck.

The kid was gone.

Foraging

Medical Center, Deep River Junction, Vermont
June 17th, 1 p.m.

He was surprised at the depth of his disappointment. It was a little late for regrets, but he realized that he had instantly come to like the boy. It occurred to him that the lad could have wandered off for a moment, and might still be nearby, but he dared not call out for him.

When he checked the front seat of the truck, he was both gratified and saddened to find that the boy had taken only a couple of cans of stew. He was gratified, because it revealed that the boy had integrity and self-control, but saddened, because he would gladly have done far more for him.

He made one more trip to the hospital kitchen from which he moved several more cartons of food to the truck, but when he started to load them, he became concerned that the springs were sagging, and regretfully left them sitting on the loading dock.

Well, maybe the kid will come back and find them, he thought.

Then he made several trips to the hospital linen storage area where he picked up two twin bed mattresses, several pillows, linens, and a stack of blankets. They didn't weigh anywhere near as much as the canned goods, and when he raised the canvas on the passenger side of the load, and jammed them around the cartons of food, he effectively prevented everything from sliding around the pickup bed. He again tied down the canvas, regretting that he couldn't afford any more weight.

He sat quietly, listening intently for any nearby activity, and hoping the boy would return. After a half hour, he heard the last of the big trucks roar north. Time seemed to drag, but he forced himself to wait another fifteen minutes before giving up on the teen. Then he realized that he was in no hurry because he did not want to overtake the convoy of trucks if they happened to be traveling up Route 19. He wandered through the hospital basement one last time, then returned to the truck.

He took a moment to walk around the rig, and noticed that one tie-down was loose. After securing it, he got in, started the engine, and drove slowly back into the deserted community, deeply concerned about the weight of the load he was putting on the old truck.

It was obvious that the scavengers with the big trucks had been after food and fuel. Every grocery market, drug store, and gas station he passed had been plundered, their doors hanging open, their plate glass windows shattered.

Wanton destruction! Don't these fools realize that these buildings would have been invaluable to a recovering population? Do they have any idea what industrial capacity it takes to roll one plate glass window?

He wondered where they were taking their loot, and imagined they were moving it to different areas, maybe hiding it in other cellars like the one he'd discovered at the co-op. He thought about that co-op, only a few miles from the entrance to Hidden Valley. It must have been where Sennett went for the grain to feed his animals the night the war started, and where he and his friend must have seen the mushroom cloud produced by the nuclear weapon that was detonated over Boston.

As CC drove through the town, he watched for any place he might scavenge tools and equipment. He stopped at a small electrical supply store where he found a book by a master electrician on how to install generator systems. Then he gathered several coils of cable, circuit breakers, switches, receptacles, work-boxes, and the like. The truck sagged dangerously under the load. With regrets, he sorted through these new treasures and again unloaded several cartons of food, leaving them behind.

The sun would set at about 6:30, but it was already growing dark under the cover of the trees that shadowed the highway. He dared not expose himself by driving with lights on after dark, but he refused to remain in the city with its lingering smells and memories of death.

He was beginning to identify something in his nature that made him always want to be moving on, to be somewhere other than the place he found himself. It was almost a compulsion, not always pleasant, that seemed to be driving him throughout his new life.

It wasn't simply wanderlust, nor a perpetual seeking after a prize. He realized he enjoyed the journey for the sake of the adventure itself. He liked to discover new things, develop new skills, and overcome unique challenges. *And maybe,* he admitted to himself, *it gives me the feeling that I'm staying one step ahead of the bad guys.*

He wondered whether he'd been like that before the amnesia, or whether some trauma had changed his personality. It hardly mattered now. The only place he felt any sense of security was Hidden Valley. Anything that would take him away from the valley and from Sarah now had to be finished as quickly as possible, if at all.

He realized that he wasn't the compulsive knight, always seeking the next joust, ready to tilt with any opponent, or the woodsman for whom the hunt becomes more important than either the trophy or the evening feast that followed.

He suspected that he was now driven by fear and insecurity. He had been impressed by that text in Sennett's old Bible that spoke of the industry of the ants that labor incessantly to gather their winter food. He too felt a compulsion to prepare for any eventuality, to make hay while the sun shines, to let no grass grow under his feet, to be the early bird that gets the worm. He laughed. Many apt metaphors had come down through the centuries from those who understood the necessity of being prepared.

He realized that he did slow down from time to time. He had stopped to pick a rose from the hospital garden, a brilliant red one, and he'd slipped it through a buttonhole in his shirt. It was crushed now, but he left it there because of the color it added to his life. And perhaps for some other inexplicable reason.

CC drove carefully, keeping an eye out for anyone else on the road. He wanted to avoid any possible contact with his self-declared enemies and their repressive ersatz government.

Funny, he thought. *Several nations wanted to take control of the United States, and their pathetic little factions were fighting one another for control of limited geographic area in a war where there were really no winners.*

Several miles north of town he was overtaken with fatigue. He pulled off into an overgrown roadside picnic area and parked the truck and trailer behind some evergreens. He opened a can of stew, ate it cold, wrapped up in his sleeping bag, and spent an uncomfortable night on the truck seat.

He awoke early, imagining he'd felt the truck shake, but when he looked through the windshield, all he could see was a squirrel leaping from the hood to a low limb. It spiraled up around the trunk until it was hanging motionless behind a limb, only its head poised where it could watch CC's every move. When CC stepped down from the truck, the squirrel shook its tail very rapidly, then scampered from view.

He was annoyed to discover that the tie-down that he'd twice secured at the hospital was again loose, and he took special pains to properly fasten it.

Eager to return home, he skipped breakfast and pulled the old truck carefully onto the pavement. He did not want to risk a flat tire at this juncture. The world seemed strangely silent, the sky gray, the air heavy. The emotional depression that seemed a constant element in his post-war world returned.

He again thought of the boy, and felt badly that he'd wandered off. It was difficult to imagine him providing for himself. "There must be a million kids in the same tough spot," he said aloud. "And I may even have children of my own out there somewhere." A wave of despair swept over him.

He'd studied a map, looking for a country road that might allow him to bypass Route 19 and serve as a shortcut to the mountain. More importantly, such a road might limit the possibility of anyone spotting him. He almost missed the sign nailed to a tree, "Old Tongore Road," and had to back up in order to make the turn onto the narrow dirt road.

There were no tire tracks, so he assumed there'd been no traffic on the road since the last rain storm and perhaps not since the war began. His map indicated that this route should bring him back onto Highway 19 only a couple of miles up-hill from Hidden Valley. He grew increasingly anxious as he drew nearer home. Like the typical parent, he was worried about Sarah and imagined all sorts of terrible things that might have happened to her.

The closer he drew to his secret valley, the greater the danger associated with his detection. If he were chased, he could not outrun a pursuer, and his location and direction would almost certainly lead them to his destination. And if he drove on past the entrance to the valley in an effort to confuse his pursuers, there was little chance he would be able to return because he would probably be apprehended.

A Wild Ride

Between Deep River Junction and the Valley

Central Vermont

June 18th, 7 a.m.

The old truck was clattering along in third gear, the right front wheel shaking, and he was afraid to push the speed above twenty. The engine began to overheat so he stopped by a stream and spent a precious half hour pouring water over the radiator to cool it down before he could safely remove the cap and refill it. This was the second time that day he'd had to top it off.

He should have reached home in a couple of hours, but after a night out he was still little better than halfway there. To make things worse, his head throbbed. This was a holdover from his fall from the cliff, and perhaps the earlier auto accident, and he sometimes wondered if he would ever heal. It frightened him, and he tried not to think about it.

He looked down for a moment to check the map, trying to determine how much further he would have to follow this route. While he tried to focus on the map, the truck started drifting toward a rocky embankment on the right. Looking up just in time, he yanked the wheel to the left, and felt a sense of relief as the truck missed the embankment, then realized that he'd escaped that danger only to run over a pile of sharp rocks. When the front right tire blew, the steering wheel spun violently, and one of the spokes slammed against his thumb almost breaking it. Foot on the brake, the truck came to an abrupt stop.

Climbing down to survey the damage, he saw that the tire was shredded. Weary and disgusted with himself, he realized that the engine had also overheated again. Well, let's look on the bright side, he thought. By the time I change the tire, it ought to have cooled down enough for me to pour water into the radiator. He looked around. There were no streams in sight, but he did have a case of bottled water laying on the cab floor. There was no help for it. He'd have to use that.

The spare tire was mounted beneath the bed of the truck, and he was gratified to realize that if it had been a rear tire that had blown, the truck would have settled so much that he wouldn't have had enough clearance to crawl under to reach the spare wheel and tire. As it was, he was nervous about lying underneath and hammering the rusted wing nuts that held the cross member supporting the spare. He was glad that he had at least put a hydraulic jack on the cab floor before leaving the valley. Favoring his uninjured hand, he was able to chock the wheels, raise the front end, and change the tire. He couldn't use his sprained thumb to hold the tire wrench, and had to put one foot on the spinner's cross member in order to break the lug nuts free.

Filling the radiator also proved a daunting task because he had to grip each water bottle between his knees while trying to unscrew the infernal little bottle tops with his good hand. And when he was all finished, he realized that water was still spraying out through a hole in the lower radiator hose.

He remembered loading a small carton of nylon stockings that he had thought would be useful for filtering paint for spraying. They might come in handy now. Ripping open the carton, he went back to the engine compartment and clumsily wrapped a stocking around the burst radiator hose, pulling the gap tightly closed and struggling with one hand to secure it with a good knot.

By the time he was finished refilling the system, it was growing dark under the trees. His thumb still throbbed fiercely, and he was afraid to drive in the dark for fear he'd blow another tire. He'd just used his only spare.

Another day wasted! he thought.

He reached into his box of food, opened the first can he reached, and barely tasting it, ate a cold supper. Then he wrapped himself up in his blankets, curled up on the seat, and fell into a restless sleep.

When he awoke, the road was shrouded in fog, but as soon as there was sufficient light to see, he started the engine and began driving slowly toward home. He had begun his ascent into the mountains. The road twisted its tortuous way along the shallower slopes, a veritable cow's path, winding back and forth and up and down.

At the moment, he was driving almost due east, and the glare of the rising sun in the swirling fog made it nearly impossible to keep his eyes open. Suddenly, as though it had burst from the center of the sun, a small airplane swept toward him. Engine roaring, it dove so low that CC had an impulse to slam on the brakes to avoid a head on collision.

He was so frightened that he almost lost control of the truck, and he could feel the hair stand up on his arms. He was ashamed of his inability to control his fear, but found himself shaking uncontrollably, his breath coming in gasps. Facing oncoming automobiles would be bad enough, but having a plane roar down at him perhaps twenty feet above the highway was terrifying. Still his thinking was clear enough.

It was smart of them to fly out of the sun, he thought, in a futile attempt to normalize his senses.

The road now ran through a valley alongside a stream, and the tall forest trees spread endlessly uphill on both sides, hopefully cramping the plane's freedom of movement. It had disappeared as quickly as it had come, the noise of its engine swallowed up by the lush forest growth.

Then suddenly it was back, and by now his adrenaline was flowing. "The time for detached musing is over," he spoke into thin air, sounding far more unruffled than he felt. He could see the plane diving at him. A man leaned out of a window cradling something in his arms. Gouts of dust began exploding where bullets tattooed a path up the middle of the road, and CC heard the stuttering of a submachine gun. Realizing that those same bullets would leave neat, well-spaced holes right up the center of his truck's windshield, he slammed the transmission down into second gear, yanked the wheel over, and slid onto the narrow, rock strewn shoulder to take advantage of the meager cover offered by the overhanging branches.

1. He couldn't stop or turn back. Even if he were lucky enough to reach the state highway, he would be like a rat in a maze, with the mountain rising on his left and the sheer cliff falling off to his right, unable to turn either left or right, and no cover to hide his movement as he turned into his secret cut in the mountainside. So even if they didn't manage to stop him with that machine gun, unless they were low on fuel they'd simply fly over the escarpment and pick him up as he drove into Hidden Valley.

CC slammed on the brakes and skidded the lumbering truck and its heavy trailer into a small clearing that had opened up beneath the trees. Leaping from the cab, he ran into the road where he could see a patch of sky through a break in the overhanging branches. He could hear the plane returning for the third time. They had reversed their approach, and were now coming from the west.

It was a mistake. The rising sun was now obscuring their vision. He drew his handgun from its holster, grasped it firmly in both hands, balanced on his feet, and aimed up through the branches. His pounding heart and shaking hands made him laugh at the possibility of hitting the racing plane with a 45 automatic.

Being able to laugh at himself, however, served to settle him down a bit. It was a forlorn hope, but he had little alternative than to rapidly squeeze off his seven rounds, aiming for the center of the propeller blades, hoping somehow to disable the low-flying aircraft. Even holding it with two hands, the pistol's kick re-awoke the pain in his sprained left thumb.

The plane appeared undamaged, but unfortunately his firing had served to attract the pilot's attention and reveal his position. Two seconds after he'd fired his last round, CC was throwing himself into a ditch, trying to dodge the return fire. Bullets ricocheted in a terrifying pattern about him.

He lay there, shaking with fear, but as his breath steadied, he became increasingly angry that these men could take upon themselves the power of life and death over a complete stranger. *They're trying to kill me,* he thought, *and they don't know who I am any more than I do.*

He was steadier now, the fear replaced by a cold, implacable anger. He thought that if all else failed, he might sneak away on foot across the mountain, but that would mean leaving the generator behind, and he realized that he was too stubborn to abandon it. It seemed to him that this obstinacy was likely to prove fatal, but he didn't have time to settle an internal debate over his own mental stability. He just wanted to somehow smash the clowns in that airplane.

He was reminded of his nearly empty handgun, and reached into his pocket for another magazine. It took just a moment to release the one and insert the other. But it was painfully difficult to pull the slide back, and he was grateful to finally see the cartridge slip into the chamber.

He had, he thought, one thing in his favor. The pilot didn't have room to land here, so he'd have to call in help that would necessarily arrive by car or truck. CC figured that he had at least fifteen minutes to clear the area, but he didn't want to leave until he knew the plane had departed so that the pilot couldn't see which direction he'd taken.

He ran back under the trees, all the while searching through the branches for the plane. Sunlight filtered through the newly-opened leaves, their lacy fabric framing the small patch of sky above his head. He wondered what to do next. He could hear the plane circling. He had recognized it as an old Cessna 180, a great two-place aircraft. The pilot was flying in slow circles obviously trying to pinpoint his location.

He had no idea where to go. He didn't even have a map or a compass, and he finally acknowledged that he had no hope of salvaging the generator, the truck, or its precious contents. He jogged back to the passenger door of the pickup, grabbed his backpack, crossed to the north side of the road, and turned in a complete circle, trying to figure out what direction might lead him through the forest and back to his little valley.

At that moment he heard the plane returning, and looked up in time to realize that the pilot was attempting a landing. He suddenly pictured little Sarah alone and waiting for him, maybe forever. It no longer mattered which direction he chose, he just had to get away from here.

As he turned to take one last disappointed look at the generator, his eyes were drawn to the back of the pickup where one corner of the tightly stretched canvas covering was suddenly bulging upward. Had a raccoon gotten into the load?

Sharp Shooter
Old Tongore Road

Central Vermont
June 18th, 7:20 a.m.

That thought was dispelled when he saw the sunlight reflected from the blade of a knife being plunged up through the bulging canvas. The blade sawed from side to side, opening the fabric, and then someone's head and arms suddenly appeared.

Through his amazement, CC heard the plane passing over, and turned quickly to follow its movements. Then his eyes were drawn back toward the truck. In the glare of the morning sun, he could just make out someone jumping over the tailboard. It was the boy from town, holding his useless rifle.

So that's where he disappeared, CC thought.

He didn't have any more time to think about the kid because the plane had turned back. It looked like his judgment had been wrong. The pilot appeared to be trying to try to land on the short level stretch of road near where he was hiding. The pilot had the plane trimmed back, flaps down, and was nearing stalling speed, ready for touchdown. It was a narrow road, barely wide enough for the wingtips to clear the trees, but the pilot obviously knew his business.

And now that guy with the machine gun is going to get a great shot at us, CC realized. He yelled at the boy to run, then dashed for a large boulder he'd spotted further back in the woods.

This kid being here changes everything, he thought. *I won't be able to get away so easily now, with or without the truck.*

He heard the sharp crack of a rifle, and again dove and rolled, waiting for the impact. Then he remembered that most bullets travel faster than sound, and that he would never hear the one that had his name on it. He also realized that he had heard only a single shot — not the rat-a-tat of the machine gun, and he turned in confusion to see why not.

Events seemed to be moving in slow motion. The plane was now less than a hundred feet downwind, moving just above stall speed. The gunner was still leaning out the co-pilot's window, machine gun in hand, but instead of firing, he was trying to get his weapon back into the plane. He was jerking on the sling, but the gun was caught across the window frame. The plane passed into a shadow cast by the mountain, and the windshield no longer reflected the sun's glare.

It was fractured, with a star-burst of cracks, like a spider's web, radiating out from a tiny central hole. The pilot, his face a mask of blood, was slumped forward over the stick. The gunner, leaning out the window, had released his weapon, then pulled his arms back into the plane, as the gun dropped toward the surface of the road. He appeared to be struggling to pull the wounded pilot back off the controls, but by the time he succeeded the wings of the plane were barely ten feet above the road.

As he turned to grab his set of controls, the pilot's body again tipped forward against the wheel. The plane's nose dipped, the port wing dropped, and the wing tip just barely touched the surface of the road. It was enough. There was a scraping, grinding noise, and the wing twisted and buckled, breaking free from the fuselage, while the plane cartwheeled into the trees across the road.

CC was diving for the protection of the boulder just as the fuel tank exploded. *I can't stand much more of this,* he thought, studying the bloody fingertips that he'd just used to examine a bump on his forehead. Nonetheless, he was back on his feet and in the cab of the truck, gunning the engine, before the explosion had finished echoing down the canyon.

He skidded the truck to a stop beside the stunned boy and yelled, "Get in!" The boy just stood there, the rifle in his hands forgotten, tears streaming down his cheeks.

CC shouted again, "Get in!"

Instead of obeying, the boy held the rifle out to him, then took off up the road in the direction from which the plane had approached. CC couldn't understand his strange behavior until he saw the boy bend down, scoop up the machine gun, and race back toward the truck. Then he turned to look at the burning plane where he could see the two bodies within engulfed in flame.

"Hurry," he shouted. "Get into the truck!"

The boy turned slowly, blinking his eyes to clear them of tears, obviously trying to comprehend what was being demanded of him. CC fought to keep the hysteria out of his own voice, "Hurry up! Get in the truck. Now!"

CC's side of the truck was closest to the plane. The wreckage was burning so fiercely that the heat would soon blister the paint on his door or ignite the canvas that covered the load in the back, and he was afraid they would be killed if they didn't get away immediately.

The boy jogged around the front of the truck, opened the passenger door, yanked out a stack of bedding, and threw it onto the load in the back. A blanket tumbled unnoticed to the ground, as, machine gun in hand, the boy climbed up beside him. He perched on the remaining goods, then looked across at CC, a queer, half-challenging, half-frightened expression on his face.

No time for conversation. The pilot had probably called for help, and CC didn't plan to be part of a charred pile of refuse when others arrived. He popped the clutch dangerously as he shoved the stick into first, and tore the soft ground as the truck lurched slowly forward. Giving it all the RPMs he felt it could stand, he gunned the old engine, slamming the transmission through the gears. The pickup was doing about fifteen on the steep incline, and the engine was winding up and skipping so badly that it sounded as though it might throw a rod.

He held it in third gear, steering wheel vibrating, engine screaming, the needle on the temperature gauge again heading for the pin. The kid, still weeping, stared at his rifle as though it was a serpent.

**A Preview of Book Three
"The Chronicles of CC
Freemen Shall Stand"**

Book 3: Return to Hidden Valley

Old Tongore Road
Central Vermont
June 18th, 7:30a.m.

It was the specter of pursuing assassins that spurred CC on. It seemed to take forever to get up that mountain, though it was probably no more than ten minutes.

The dirt road unexpectedly intersected with the mountain highway, and he slid around the corner onto the blacktop without slowing for the stop sign. The engine was beginning to knock, and steam curled from under the hood as the decrepit truck heaved itself around the last curve before reaching the crest of the mountain road.

The kid was shouting at him above the sound of the wind and the engine. "Mister, did you see the markings on that old plane? A big star and four small ones. Those guys must have been Russians."

"Russians?" CC turned to look at the boy. "The Russians have a single red star. Those markings were Chinese. Don't they teach you anything in school?"

"Yeah, sure," was the sarcastic response. "School's great."

CC regretted his caustic question.

"The yellow stars on a red field is the Chinese flag."

"The markings might have been Chinese," the boy countered, "but those guys in the cockpit weren't. They were Americans!" He started to cry again. "I killed Americans."

CC realized that he sounded callous when he responded, "So what?" He was not insensitive to the boy's pain, but those guys had been trying to kill them, and an enemy is an enemy. Obviously the rumors he'd heard were true. The Chinese were among those who were trying to take over.

But America is a lot of country to take over, he thought, *and many Americans who have survived are showing themselves to be pretty tough customers. Maybe taking over the USA won't be as easy as our numerous enemies had assumed.*

He turned to the boy. "The Chinese have been preparing for war for decades. They had plenty of money, the world's largest army, and a technologically advanced navy and air force. They probably invaded a number of countries. It's my guess that in spite of their stealing many of our military and industrial secrets, and our business and political leaders giving or selling them a lot more, when push came to shove, some of our military still gave them a bad time."

The kid merely stared at him.

"The point is," CC said patiently, "that maybe the Chinese won't be able to supply enough troops and equipment to pacify all the countries they've invaded. Unless, of course, they can blackmail, brainwash, intimidate, and bribe the local populations to work for them."

"Maybe so," the boy responded, "but they sure did '...blackmail, brainwash, intimidate, or bribe..' the two guys in that plane."

"Yes, they certainly did," CC agreed. "And that's why you must not feel guilty about defending yourself against them."

The truck was rolling down a short steep grade, and CC pulled the wheel gently to guide the old truck around the broad turn. When he'd cleared the crest and was completing the short distance to his turnoff, CC drew to a stop and put the truck in neutral to let the wind cool the idling engine.

He pulled a dark stocking cap from his pack on the seat and said to the boy, "Put this on." The lad seemed reluctant, so CC repeated himself. This time the boy obeyed him, pulling the knit hat down to his hair line. CC told him to pull it down over his face so that he couldn't see. The kid looked at him in distrust, but again he obeyed.

"Put your hands on the dashboard and brace yourself," CC commanded. The boy stretched out one arm to grasp the molded contour of the dashboard, used the other to grasp the armrest of the door, and spread his feet on the floor, his legs straddling a carton.

CC did not see anyone on the road or in the air, but he waited until he'd reached his turn before braking violently. Sliding the battered vehicle around, they bounced heavily across the swale, for he was intent on vanishing quickly, whatever the cost to the truck and generator trailer. That was almost his undoing, as the trailer bounced from wheel to wheel, almost flipping over.

Pulling beneath the trees, CC slipped the transmission into neutral, set the brake, and told the boy to stay put while he ran back to scuff out any tracks. He took particular pains because he knew that pursuit was inevitable and he feared that his new enemies would somehow discover that he'd entered the valley.

He didn't want to think about the burned bodies in the plane's wreckage, but he couldn't help hoping that the pilot was so sure of himself that he hadn't called in to report their contact, and that the damage would be so extensive that any search party would assume they had crashed as a result of a malfunction.

As he swept the ground with a dead tree branch, CC thanked God there had been no rain, and that the leaves were dry. He left no evidence of his passing but for a small tree that he'd sideswiped in passing, leaving a splintered branch with a white scar, almost invisible to a searching eye. As usual, he rubbed the raw wood with soil, dropped the dead limb next to it, then took a can of black pepper from his pocket and sprinkled the entire can around the area. That should slow down any hounds they might put on our scent, he thought.

Just as he returned to the safety of the trees, he heard a roar, and looked out across the valley to see a low-flying helicopter, the five red stars unmistakable on its fuselage, heading across the mountain toward the cloud of smoke which rose from the downed plane's wreckage. The copter was gone before its potential malice registered on him. These people certainly appeared to have the necessary ordinance to subdue a stricken and passive society.

Once again, he slid behind the wheel, knowing the truck wasn't going much further, and began to plead with God to keep it running. He had been destroying a lot of motor vehicles lately. They reached the small lake and he again stopped the truck under the trees.

He told the boy to remove his mask, then got down to try to pour water into the radiator. He had left the cap loose so that it wouldn't build up pressure and scald him if he needed to remove it again. The engine had almost died, but when he poured water in, and poured more over the radiator, it cooled down and the engine slowed its frightening clatter.

The boy just sat there. He seemed to be stunned by the mystery of the canyon. CC wondered whether he was held in the thrall of its beauty, or traumatized by the occurrences of the past twenty minutes. Still worried about pursuit, CC ran back toward the highway to see whether they had been followed. He was still well back from the road when a state police car, siren wailing, roared up the hill and disappeared in the direction of the plane crash.

Get your copy of "Freemen Shall Stand"

Amazon

Apple

Barnes and Noble

 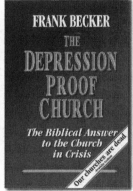

Also from Frank Becker, two great non-fiction books
You Can Triumph Over Terror

Special Agent Frank Gil (Retired) FECR PD; featured on COPS, Metro-Dade Special Response Team (SWAT) wrote: "Frank's book should be required reading. By preparing, you increase your chances of survival, facilitate our ability to assist you, and reduce your own stress and anxiety."

John, Sipos, Broadcast Journalist and host of "Hour Tampa Bay," wrote, "If you apply the ideas in this book...you and your family will radically improve your prospects for survival."

Get it your copy of *Triumph Over Terror* now!

The Depression Proof Church: The Biblical Answer to the Church in Crisis

Paige Patterson — past president of the Southern Baptist Convention, and president of America's largest seminary — wrote: "In a day of 'how-to' manuals on church growth and effectiveness, to find a writer who tells the truth...is a breath of fresh air.... Frank Becker...has clearly enunciated the one essential, namely, a return to the church of the New Testament."

And Dr. John Kenzy — who co-founded the Teen Challenge Bible Institute with David Wilkerson — called The Depression Proof Church "Compelling and timely," and said that it "exposes revelation from God."

Senator Stephen R. Wise, PhD, called it "hard hitting," "inspiring a return to biblical practices that have been forsaken in a lust for ever larger churches."

And the Jacksonville Theological Seminary created a course called, The Depression Proof Church, for students at every level.

Get the believer's primer for end time events...
The Depression Proof Church

The Chronicles of CC

The Star Spangled Banner Series

War's Desolation
The Heav'n Rescued Land
Freemen Shall Stand
Our Cause It Is Just
Conquer We Must

Visit CC's Blog

www.FrankBecker.com

Favorite "WarsDesolation" on Twitter

Like "WarsDesolation" on Facebook

Made in the USA
Charleston, SC
31 August 2016